D0627161

# KIT O'BRIEN

# KIT O'BRIEN

by

## Edgar Lee Masters

BONI & LIVERIGHT
1927

## NOTE

I have chosen Petersburg for the locale of Kit O'Brien because it grows out of *Mitch Miller*, where the scene of that story is laid, and where this one carries on to further conclusions. Wherever there is expressed here any criticism of the characters placed upon the stage of Petersburg, or upon the civilization portrayed as belonging to it, I ask the reader to shift his imagination to the American small town in general, and not to Petersburg in literalness. I love that town of my boyhood, its people and its ways too deeply to dispraise them, or to say anything but good of them.

E. L. M.

# KIT O'BRIEN

# KIT O'BRIEN

## CHAPTER I

"YOU see George Montgomery was married while I was gone, which don't make no diffrence with this here story, except that it was awful nice to have a woman as good as Eliza White around his house, which was the woman he married. They had been goin' together for years, to church and things; and ridin' about in his buggy in the spring when George was goin' out to the maple grove to tend to the buckets when the sap was flowin'. I had seen this when I was runnin' around with George Heigold and Charley King, not with Mitch Miller, who got kilt on the train,

1

because we was never very good friends. He knocked my teeth out onct with knucks made of a log chain link, and that made us not very good friends.

"Everyone says that George married Eliza because after his pap died he had that big brick house and no one to take care of it, cook or nothin'; and he had lots of business on account of lots of land which he got from his pap when he died. George's pap was old Jeff Montgomery, that owned that lot where they built the new schoolhouse. I played there lots; and onct we was there, a lot of us boys and a boy named Peter Bennett, the funniest boy I ever heard talk; and we was afeard old Jeff would come along and shoo us out of the lot. He didn't want his cows bothered, and was awful stingy. So this here Peter Bennett was talkin' about old Jeff, and he says, 'old Jeff comes here and throws a grain of corn and a spear of grass to his cows and says, there now eat till you bust.' You orter heard the boys laugh and me. Well, George was not this here way, but was awful generous, and let us have sap when we wanted it, and would give us a chew off his honey-bee

2

plug, and take us ridin' to his pap's farms.

"I don't know why George went away to Dakota, or maybe it was Sasscatchewon, but he did, and that's where he was when his pap died. So George inherited, bein' the only livin' child, and come back to look after the big brick house and the farms. He didn't marry Eliza right away, and I don't know why he married her at all except that she is a awful nice woman; but they might have gone on jest as they did for so many years before, her livin' at her pap's house across the street and him livin' in the house his pap willed him, and goin' about together as they allus did, except for George's cookin', and clothes and such like. But before they married this is what happened: George was forty-five, a old man, but lookin' the same as ever, and he had a woman named Mary to keep house for him, which was not a good housekeeper. I heard this and Eliza told me so too, after I got back, and she said that she had told George the same. But she run into things she didn't like any better than she liked this woman Mary, which was a girl named Cora Dunleavy, which George had

3

took from the House of the Good Shepherd; and a feller named Joe Lester who was a pickpocket, that the prison had turned over to George to watch, and if he was good he could live with George, but if he did any bad things again he would have to go back to prison. Eliza was afeard that this Joe Lester would kill George sometime, and she didn't like the way Mary kept house for George; so she was talkin' this to George, and that's how I think they got married. But it made no diffrence. Joe Lester and this Cora Dunleavy went right on livin' with George after he married Eliza, and of course Joe could have kilt George as well after Eliza come to the house to live as before. I don't see no sense in this. And besides after George and Eliza was married they took a trip to California for a weddin' trip, leavin' Cora and Joe right in the house, where Joe could have stole anything he wanted. But Eliza told me that when she got back everything was there, not a thing missin', and the house all clean and nice ready for George and she.

"George could never get enough of company, nor do enough for people, and so when

4

they was comin' back and stopped in St. Louis, George had picked up a old school friend named Ernest Drew, a poet and not worth a pinch of salt, as pap would say. And so when I got back to Petersburg that night, and went to George's house, not knowin' he was married, but only knowin' that he was back from Dakota or wherever it was, because I saw lights in the house, and saw him movin' around in the rooms; and suspectin' that old Jeff was dead or somethin' on account of seein' so many in the rooms movin' about too, because old Jeff was too stingy to have anyone in his house; so havin' come back this way I found when I got in the house that this Cora Dunleavy was there, and Joe Lester and this Ernest Drew, besides Eliza which had married George, as I saw. They was all makin' wine together and I heard George call Eliza honey right at first so I knew somethin' had happened. But I am gettin' ahead of my story; for why I went away and how I come to come back to Petersburg comes first.

"I took terrible chances in comin' back to Petersburg, on account of the terrible state's

attorney they had there, and not knowin'
what had happened to George Heigold and
Charley King. For if I had knowed they
had been sent to prison while I was gone, I
wouldn't have come back for Judith Siddons
or anybody else. That's why when I got
back that night all in the dark to Petersburg
I began to sneak around George's house, and
not to go to my pap's who would have turned
me over to the sheriff, as like as not. Why, I
was so tickled I didn't know what to do when
I saw George's face through the winder, and
knew that even if old Jeff was around George
would do the best for me, and maybe keep
me out of jail.

"You see I didn't go right into George's
house at first, or try to. I went sneakin'
around, once lyin' down in the grass, and
watchin' the light over in Judith Siddons'
big house where I had delivered her all safe
after that long ride that I'll tell about.
Judith's old mother had come to the door,
and some servants, while I stood in the shad-
der of the porch and wasn't known, and heard
her mother cry and go on like mad because
Judith had come back. When I heard the

6

old woman ask Judith where she come from, and how she got here, and heard Judith fib about it, because she knew that I didn't want anyone to know I was in Petersburg, I skinned out, and went over to George's yard, kind of from habit, and then findin' the good luck of George bein' back as I have told.

"Judith's mother didn't know her, and nobody would except by her voice—but that belongs later to my story. Well, as I said, I didn't go into George's house at once; it must have been half a hour that I walked around and lay in the grass all cold and covered with dew, because it was fall. But finally I went up to the back porch where I could see all these people and George workin' at somethin', liftin', pourin' and all that. Pretty soon as I was standin' in the corner of the porch gettin' ready to knock maybe and get in, Eliza opened the door suddently, and said, 'I thought I heard something.' She looked all around, and finally seein' the light over to Judith Siddons, she said, 'Ain't that funny that the Seward house is all lighted up?' And that was the first that I knowed that her name was Judith Seward and not Judith Sid-

7

dons; and besides her real name was Julia and
not Judith. So Eliza said, 'Maybe old Mrs.
Seward has died, George. You'd better go
over and see if you can do anything.'
George then come to the door and he said,
'That is funny, I believe I will go over.' So
then he turned in and Eliza closed the door;
and pretty soon he come out with his hat and
coat on and went over to the Seward house in
a hurry. George bein' gone I dasent knock
and go in or try to for I didn't know what
Eliza would do, so there I stayed waitin' for
George to come back, and sittin' under the
winder wrapped in some old carpet to keep
warm. I was almost willin' to run down to
the Fillmore woods and sleep in the leaves and
then next mornin' walk to St. Louis again
where I had gone, as I'll tell later. While I
waited this here way, I heard George's voice
talkin' to Eliza and the rest, as he had come
back and come in by the front door. So
it was awful interestin' for it was about Judith Siddons. George said, 'Well, won't that
beat the world. I thought Julia was in South
America and here she is over at her mother's
house, and no one knows how she got back

8

here. There ain't no train at this hour and the hired girl says that Julia jest came.' I almost snickered hearin' this. Then George went on speakin' to this here poet Ernest, who didn't know about things in Petersburg: 'Julia ain't been here much for years. Her father was one of the most prominent men here, and pretty well off onct and used to give her everythin', and so spoiled her. He was awful proud when she was about fourteen and the champion roller skater here, and was in local plays. He sent her away to school, and humored her in every way; but when she wanted to be a actress he got scared; and finally when she ran away with a troupe he was almost heart-broke. After a while she came back, and everybody treated her mean; and so she acted more outlandish, maybe, than she would otherwise, and always had men around drivin' and in the hammock and sech like. They knowed she had took the name of Judith Siddons, and when the actor came here which was the star in the troupe that she had run off with there was lots of talk. Old man Seward was kind of down in the mouth, knowin' the talk; and he went

9

around showin' clippin's from newspapers where Julia had been praised for actin', and as everybody loved her father they pretended to believe that Julia had made a hit, because they was so sorry for him.' Then Eliza spoke up and says, 'She couldn't act at all, and she couldn't sing; and as for the rest I think that Julia deserves no better fate than Cora, bein' the same kind of a nature.' By this I thought Cora must have stepped out of the kitchen for a minute or else Eliza wouldn't speak so plain. Then George began again: 'They never believed here that Julia could act, not even when they saw that she was written up in the Chicago papers. And when she come back here in the summers they treated her awful mean, the church people did, and kind of smiled and sneered about her actin', and said bad things about her life, her marriages and all that; for first she married a cornet player, and brought him back here; and Judith's father tried to start him in business. When she come back next summer or the next she had a rich man from New York for a husband.' 'That's what her father said,' said Eliza. 'I think it's true,'

10

said George. Then George went on: 'And so after a few years she didn't come back; and I wonder what made her ever come back at all, unless it's the old story of wantin' to be received by your home people, and have them recognize that you have struck it, when you get instead only stares and snubs.' 'What do you expect?' said Eliza. 'She never sang but one song or maybe two, that one "When Other Lips and Other Hearts," and "Within a Mile of Edinboro Town"; and she couldn't sing. We had her at our Musical here onct when she was back, and received her as well as we could; and everybody could see that she couldn't sing. Which bein' so why all this talk of New York, and goin' about the country and gettin' married every little bit, and havin' newspaper notices?' 'They was about actin',' says George. 'Well,' says Eliza, 'she couldn't act any better than she could sing, and I know it.' 'She sang for a benefit here,' said George. 'And that time when she was back she did everything to be friends with people, and she gave money to charity, and was as good as she could be; and they treated her like a criminal.

11

I think it's mean. And now that she's back I'm goin' to do everything I can for her.' 'Well,' says Eliza, 'I think you'd better give up your other business and jest take care of the failures and the outcasts. Pretty soon you're off to Pontiac to get George Heigold and Charley King out of the Reformatory; and by that time Kit O'Brien will turn up somewhere at the other end of the country and you'll have to go to him . . . and where do I come in?' 'You never get out,' says George; and I thought I heard him kiss Eliza, for Eliza laughed as if her mouth was smothered or somethin'. But I was awful down in the mouth now, and cold and hungry, and if I didn't get to stay at George's and be welcomed by Eliza what would I do? Still, George went on with awful interestin' talk and I forgot my troubles. He was sayin' that he had been talkin' that day to the state's attorney and told him that it was a shame to send boys like George and Charley to prison who had done nothin' but steal a pie; and that the state's attorney had said that law is law, and that when they got out of prison they will respect the law,

and that they would never get out until they
had served their sentences, if he had anything
to say about it. Here my heart give a jump;
for I was just as guilty of stealin' that pie
as George and Charley, and maybe I was
about to be caught and sent to prison, too.
George went on sayin' what the state's attorney said, which was that you can't have
a gov'ment unless the law is enforced, but
only arnachy; and Eliza spoke up and said
'that's right,' so then George kissed her
again, I believe, and they all laughed. Then
George went on to tell a story that I knowed
nothin' about and which knocked me cold,
which was about Mitch Miller; and was that
Mitch did not get kilt because of a numb
foot which dragged against the wheel of the
car without his knowin' it, but that he was
knocked under the wheels by the brakeman
who caught him flippin'; and that George
Heigold and Charley King had been paid
by a lawyer in town who was for the railroad not to tell how Mitch got kilt, for fear
Mr. Miller would sue the railroad; and that
then the railroad lawyer to make it sure that
George and Charley could never tell what

13

they knowed and after that pie was stole, had taken hold of that and sent 'em to the Reformatory, and so got 'em out of the way. Well, wouldn't they want me out of the way, too, thinkin' I knowed about Mitch? And I could see that what we knowed was worse for us than eatin' the stole pie. By this time George was talking' about hisself. He was sayin' that there ain't a boy that hain't stole somethin', and that he had stole hisself, watermelons and apples; and that onct he had stole from Cave Sanford, the old grocer-man who was awful watchin' and stingy; that he stole a cornelian marble from him onct and was glad of it to this day; and that he could feel now just as he felt when he stood by the front window when old Cave was waitin' on a customer; and suddenly flipped the cornelian up his sleeve and after-wards walked back to old Cave and bought some Arbuckle's coffee for which he had been sent by his pap, that old Jeff Montgomery that I have spoke of. And how proud he was that he fooled old Cave, and asked for the coffee without crackin' a smile; and how a few days later he went in to buy

14

somethin' else from old Cave and heard him
talkin' to another old feller about that cornelian marble; and tellin' him that he believed he had mixed it with some commies
and sold it not thinkin' to some boy dishonest
enough not to come back and say, 'Here,
Mr. Sanford, this cornelian does not belong
to me.' And that if the boy had done that
he would have rewarded him with a stick of
white gum for bein' an honest boy and pre-
parin' to be a honest man. George was
sayin' that it made him laugh to-day to
think about old Cave, and how much he de-
served to have that cornelian hooked, seein'
that old Cave would fool you when weighin'
butter or measurin' coffee, if he could do
it without your seein' him.

"Then another voice spoke up, and it was
Joe Lester's as I knowed afterward, and
he said: 'I got my first send-up for stealin'
a cornelian. I was only eight years old;
my father was a drunk and had died, and
my mother left me a lot with an old aunt
while she was away tryin' to make a livin'.
It was down in Tennessee. There was a
woman in the town named Anna Herbert

15

Harriet Howard Hayes, for she had been married that many times. She ran a store where she sold kites, toys, marbles and things; and we boys used to go in there and stand around waitin' for a chance to hook somethin', like minnows waitin' for crumbs. So one day I was in there tryin' to hook a cornelian that I wanted and had seen through the winder, and I was keepin' my eyes on the old gal, not knowin' that she was watchin' me, and was too smart for me; and jest as I flipped the cornelian she grabbed me and turned me over to the town marshal, who had arrested my father for bein' drunk a good many times; and I was tried and sent to a school. And this is what happens to you: when you get into a school like that you look forward to the Reformatory as a step-up, and when you get there you want to go to the penitentiary as a high-up college; for kids soon get filled up with dreams of bein' a big criminal after they onct get started. Before I got through I had been in eight penitentiaries and about thirty jails, until Mr. Montgomery got me out and stood by me. Now I am through

16

for good. But I'll say that the penitentiary wouldn't be so bad if it wasn't for one thing, and that is your cell-mate. If you get celled with some fool, some wild man, some dirty man, you almost go crazy, and you're afeard all the time that you'll lose your head and kill him. And all I've got to say about these two boys who stole the pie is that I hope they cell with each other if they want to; for things go in prison accordin' to the will of the warden. It is a gov'ment by itself; and there is no one to know or to care what happens. It was cell-mates more than anythin' else that made me sink lower and lower, until I took to everythin' to get worse in mind and body, to destroy myself, havin' the disposition to do this in my nature from the first, and I don't know why. You get to hate yourself more and more. I used to expose myself so as to catch cold, eat the wrong things when I could, or not eat at all. Onct I had a sore eye, and the doctor thought I was goin' to lose it. I was glad. I wanted to be blind in one eye and have the guards look at my blind eye. All of us professionals hated jails, and

17

we broke out of 'em whenever we could: but we was glad to be sent to the penitentiary. It's the real thing. You have no responsibility; you spend the time workin', and you don't need a job or have to steal. Everything is done for you. The load of livin' and wanderin' is taken off of you.'

"Then George spoke up and says: 'All this is very interestin', Joe, but I'll bet you don't want to go back to prison now.' 'No, I don't,' says Joe, 'you have showed me another life that I like better; and I don't like to think of them kids in prison for that pie, or of Kit O'Brien goin' to prison for that pie.' 'He will never go,' said George, 'never while I have a dollar.' So hearin' that and bein' so cold and hungry, I got up and knocked; and George come and opened the door. You orter to have seen his face! He blinked first, then he looked me up and down, then he took hold of me and brought me closer into the light, then he said, 'In the name of God, Kit, where did you come from?' 'From near St. Louis,' says I. By this time Ernest Drew and Joe and Cora, and Eliza, who, of course, knowed me, crowded around

18

me. I was shiverin' from the cold and because I had not et. The room was so warm
and nice and light, and smelt of grapes and
wine and fresh-made bread. So I began to
cry on my sleeve and look down, awful
shamed that I was cryin'. And pretty soon
I felt arms around me and a little hug give
me. It was Eliza. And she went and got
me some beans and bread and I fell asleep
eatin' and askin' for more beans. When I
woke up I was in bed and it was almost noon
of the next day."

## CHAPTER II

"I MUST have woke up jest at daybreak,
though as I said I didn't come clear to till
noon. I remember hearin' the jays holler
in the tops of the pine trees in George's
yard. They allus sound to me like blue sky
bustin' loose, and I don't know why, and
when the sun is shinin' gold through the
pines and the jays is hollerin' it is awful
nice. I think George must have been foolin'
around the hall waitin' for me to come to;
for I had no sooner opened my eyes for
good when the door opened and George come
in. I dreamed durin' the night of bein' in
a place where it was all boarded up and not
much air; and another time I dreamed of
runnin' away from the sheriff, and bein'
20

down on the Mississippi with Miss Siddons.
So as soon as George come in I knowed I
was all right; and his face was so smilin'
and friendly that I was happy onct again.
He come over to the bed and kind of roughed
me around a little, tickled me and fooled
that-a-way, and then he asked me if I didn't
want some breakfast, which I did as I was
awful hungry.

"He had already been out to one of his
farms, and made fun of me for sleepin' so
late; but I bet if he had drove Miss Siddons
from near St. Louis he would have been
tired, too.  So when I said I could eat all
they'd give me he went to the stair and
called in a loud voice, 'breakfast,' and as I
tried to get out of bed he come over and
pushed me back and said I could eat in
bed.  I had heard of that but had never
done it.  It wasn't no time till Cora Dunleavy
came up with eggs and milk and biscuit and
wonderful fine honey; and while I was eatin'
Eliza came in, then Ernest Drew that poet;
and finally Joe Lester come to the door to
ask George if he should take one of the
horses down to get shod by the blacksmith.

21

So he asked me how I felt and then went out.
George set around while I et, and Eliza a
little; but Cora had to work, and Ernest
wanted to read somethin'.   Now this is the
way things was up to now: George knowed
that I had helped to steal that pie; he
knowed that George Heigold and Charley
King had gone to the Reformatory for
stealin' it, because he had started to help
'em out since comin' back from California;
but he didn't know that I had anythin' to
do with Miss Siddons, or that I had drove
her back to Petersburg or anythin'.   Onct
while George was settin' there while I et,
Eliza came in and asked him how Miss Siddons was, and he said he didn't see her, that
they wouldn't let him; that she was in her
room restin'.   So not thinkin' I spoke up
and says, 'She's all right, you don't need to
worry.'   Which showed that I knowed somethin' about her, which George caught quick
and says, 'How do you know, Kit?'   So
then knowin' George and Eliza for friends,
and intendin' anyway to tell 'em all about
the pie and everythin' I jest spoke right
out: 'I brought her back here to Petersburg,'
22

says I. 'I brought her back last night.'
'From where?' said George. 'From near St.
Louis,' says I. 'And maybe you think it
wasn't a drive, and except I was so sorry
for her I'd never come back to Petersburg
and run the chance of bein' arrested and
tried. For I didn't know that you was here,
George. And after I got her out of the
wagon and up the steps, and had put the
horse in the barn I began to think for the
first what I was goin' to do. Should I sleep
in the barn, should I run out of town, or
go down to Fillmore's woods? Of course
I couldn't go to my pap. And so I stood
in the barn door and saw lights all here in
your house, and I jest had a kind of idea
that somethin' was goin' on here, and that
your pap, George, didn't have nothin' to do
with it.' 'Why?' says George. 'Because,'
says I, 'he wouldn't have so many lights
burnin' all over the house.' So George
laughed at that. And then I told him about
sneakin' around the house and lyin' in the
grass, and settin' scrooched on the porch
wrapped up in a carpet and waitin' for
somethin' to happen. Then Eliza come over

23

to me and said I needed a haircut and some
new things, and she patted me as if she kind
of liked me.  Then I asked George what
he was goin' to do about the sheriff; and
he said not to worry, but he wanted to know
all about the pie, because he said he was
goin' to get up papers right away to get
George and Charley out of the Reformatory, and he would at the same time keep
the state's attorney from sendin' me there,
if he could.  So I spoke up and says, that
they didn't care nothin' about the pie,
but they wanted to get George and Charley
out of the way for what they knowed about
Mitch Miller bein' kilt on the train, which
George and Charley knowed their own selves,
and that's why they started with me to St.
Louis; and that they thought I knowed about
Mitch, too.  Then George spoke right out,
'Kit, did you steal a pie?'  'Yes,' says I, 'I
stole a pie just as much as George and
Charley did; but since I heard you tell last
night that you had stole a cornelian of Cave
Sanford I didn't feel so bad about the pie;
and as fur as that's concerned I think I
have wiped the pie out by bringin' Miss Sid-

24

dons to her home, and runnin' the chance of the state's attorney.' George laughed and said yes. So then Ernest come in the room and set down; and there I was propped up in bed tellin' my story, with Joe Lester come back and settin' there, his pointed ears stickin' up like a dog's and his eyes so bright, and Cora Dunleavy standin' by the door, the dish towel in her hand, listenin' and neglectin' her work of gettin' dinner, which nobody had till one o'clock. So I went on to tell 'em all about everythin' from the time I left Petersburg till I brought Miss Siddons back to her house the night before, and this is the way I told it:

"You see, I knowed Charley King and George Heigold, and chummed with 'em some; and I knowed Mitch Miller, too, but we never got along. He whipped me onct, and he was the only boy who ever did; and he wouldn't except he used knucks. So we didn't run together much. But there was a story that I was near when Mitch got kilt, and knowed about it, which I didn't. But George and Charley was, and it made lots of trouble for 'em. So they wanted to go

25

away and get work sommers, and never come back. You see George is about sixteen and Charley about fifteen and I am nearly fifteen. And we all have worked; but after Mitch was kilt they didn't seem to get nothin' to do like they used to, carryin' coal and all that. But they had some money, a little, I mean, that is, George had, which he earned pickin' berries for old man Harbin. And they come to me and wanted me to go to St. Louis with 'em and get work. My ma is dead, you know, and my home is nothin' on account of pap havin' nobody to do nothin' about the house, all the girls bein' married and gone off; and so I thought I'd go to St. Louis, too; for I could sort of see that they was closin' around me on account of Mitch Miller, same as George and Charley, though I didn't know nothin' about how he got kilt and only heard. So that's the way it was.

"So we started out of town, that is separate, for I was meetin' 'em at the bridge. When we got to the store there by the coal mine, just beyond the bridge, and before you go up the hill, George said we needed some

26

cigarettes and terbacker and matches; so he went in the store, and it was about early afternoon; and he come back with the things and we went on. He ought to have bought cheese and crackers and somethin' to eat, for we was awful hungry before long; and that's what got us into trouble, bein' hungry. . . . Finally about the middle of the afternoon, or maybe later, we come down a hill, havin' before that asked the nearest town on the way to St. Louis. And there at the foot of this hill was a house, and to one side of it a hill, so that the house was kind of shut in. And we could see that nobody could see us . . . that came into my mind. But that wasn't it after all, for as I said George had some money, and he said we'd go over to this house and ask the farmer for somethin' to eat. It would soon be night and we had to take somethin' along, or beg at another place. Well, so we went to the front door, and George knocked while the rest of us stood near; and he knocked and no one come, and he knocked again. And he says that nobody's at home, or maybe they's in the back part of the house. So we all went around the house. And there was a screened porch, and a table on the porch and we could see that pie on the table. We could smell it, too, for it was coolin' off. So we knocked again, and nobody come, for there was nobody at home. Then I clumb up furder on the steps and I could see two more pies besides the one we saw first, and I says, 'There ain't only one pie, there's three.' And they looked and there they was to one side, and kind of under a paper to keep the flies off or somethin'; for it looked now as if the first pie had been under this paper and had been blowed off. So George tried the door, and it was latched on the inside, and he gave it a jerk, and it didn't come, so he jerked it again and it opened, and we stepped onto the porch and took the pie, that is George did; and so we cut it into three pieces with a knife which was there, and then we begun to eat it, for we was awful hungry with that long walk. So we et the pie. And then we thought we'd get somethin' from the cupboard to take along, meat or somethin,' for the pies was soft to carry. And just as we was goin' in the kitchen I heard

28

somethin' and looked around and saw two eyes lookin' at us through the screen porch; and then I saw four eyes; and there was two men, two farmers who had seed us when we came in the front gate. And so they made for us, callin' us burglars and town robbers and everythin'. Well, we run, you bet, run through the house and jumped through a open window in one of the bedrooms, after openin' a door into the bedroom. Somehow I got to the winder first, and got out in the yard and started to run, with these farmers after us, comin' like the dickens. I run through the open gate, but George and Charley started to climb the fence. That took more time; and the men run through the gate and around to the place where George and Charley was climbin' over. I could see that, but that was all I saw. I just run as fast as I could, and never looked back. Well, they must have had their hands full with George and Charley; for it was a hour, it seemed, before I heard again. I had run around the hill that was in front of the house, and bein' out of breath I slid down into a hole back of

29

some weeds there and jest waited to see
what would happen. After a while I heard
their voices. They had come along in their
wagon, and I could jest see through the
weeds that they had George and Charley tied
in the bottom. So I lay still, and the men
got out and looked around; and one said to
another, 'Why you lookin' here?' 'Because
this is where he disappeared around the hill.'
And the other said: 'Why, he might be a
half mile away or sommers in the woods.'
And so after lookin' around a little and
cussin' town robbers and all that, they drove
on sayin' that the sheriff would get me, as
soon as they sent him from town, after
puttin' George and Charley in jail. Then
they went on. And so I began to wonder
what to do, and just where I was. I didn't
know the country at all. I waited till it
was dark and then I began to walk, goin'
down hill mostly; and I began to think that
I must be comin' toward the river. And
about dark I come to high weeds and woods,
and I was sure I was gettin' near the Sangamon River. I stepped on about a hundred
snakes, and got into mire and had an awful

30

time; and finally I saw a bridge away off, and so I hurried, and sure enough it was the river. Then I went down to the river. It was nice moonlight now and I could see good; and there by the shore was a rowboat, and oars; and I suppose somebody hadn't left it long there. You see, stealin' the pie made me steal the boat. But I had to do somethin', and so I got in the boat and rowed down the stream under the moon with the whippoorwills singin' and the bats flyin' and everything so still and scarey. And yet it was fun, and wonderful. And so I rowed until I was tired, and fell asleep, and didn't wake up at all till the next mornin'.

"The boat had drifted to the shore and was caught under a big tree that bent over the river and almost kept you from passin' under it. It was a wonder that I didn't have my head good and bumped. So I looked around, and there on the shore there was a big snake all coiled and lickin' his hot poker tongue out, and lookin' at me. He might have bit me when I was asleep, and I could see all kinds of trouble before I got

31

to St. Louis. So I watched him and didn't do nothin'; and I began to think about eatin'. And I was thirsty, too. I couldn't guess how fur I had drifted down, and I didn't know the country at all, except that it still looked like the Sangamon River, for it was like what it was at Petersburg and Oakford, too, where I had been. I must have been lookin' off or somethin', for I saw now that the snake had gone; and just now I heard voices on the other side of the river; and I looked over that-a-way, and there was a farm, and two men plowin', which had stopped at the end of the furrow by the bank. And one said somethin' to the other about Greenview, so I knowed I was near there, which is only ten miles from Petersburg, and not much of a start on the way to St. Louis. I stood there while these men was talkin' to each other, and they didn't see me, for I was kind of scrooched down in the weeds, watchin' for the snake and watchin' the men, too. The men began to plow pretty soon, and so pickin' up a stick to kill the snake if I saw him again, I pushed through the hot stinkin' weeds to some

32

blackberry bushes, and picked a lot and et all I could. Then I come back to the river, and scooped up some water with my hands and drank; and that was my breakfast. By this time the men was comin' back to the end of the furrow by the river, and their voices was gettin' plainer: and so I waited for them to get to the end, and then to have all the time while they was goin' back to the other end to get pushed off from the shore and be down the river out of sight before they got back again to where they could see me.

"It come all right; and so I pushed off and started down the river, makin' for St. Louis, not knowin' how awful fur it was. I was pretty lonesome now and wonderin' about George and Charley, but when I thought of turnin' back I could see the sheriff waitin' for me in Petersburg, and besides if he warn't what was there for me to go back to? School would take up in the fall, and my pap hain't been very good to me, and so I was willin' to go on, though not knowin' where.

"And that afternoon, it bein' pretty hot,

I drew up for a rest on the shady side of the river, and not fur from where I stopped was a boy fishin'; and I spoke to him, and come up to where he was, and saw that he had caught some catfish; and so I asked him for one, tellin' him that I could dig bait for him, or do anything. And he said it wasn't necessary, that he had all the fish he wanted, and would give me one for nothin'. He was a nice boy. So I talked to him. And he had matches, and I made a fire, and cooked the fish and et it, with this boy lookin' at me and wonderin', I expect, who I was, and where I come from. I told him I was rowin' back down the river to where my uncle was; and he believed me, and we talked and I went on, after gettin' out of him that where we was was near Greenview. And so it went, and I was gettin' hungrier and hungrier in spite of the fish.

"But that night I got some straw and put it in the bottom of the boat and stood some bushes by the boat so no snakes could crawl in, and went to sleep. But before that I found some more berries and et 'em, and drank the water the same as before. When

I woke up I saw I couldn't stand it any longer; so I got out and walked to a farmhouse and asked for some food. She was a nice lady and told me she would give me a good breakfast if I would split and bring in some wood. So I did that, and made a big pile for her. And she gave me eggs and milk, and berries, and some boiled eggs to take with me and some bread. So I set off again all fixed on food. I took an awful chance on someone stealin' my boat; but they didn't, and so I went on down the river. Somehow I began to think about disguisin' myself for fear I'd run into someone who knew me and take me back to the sheriff. So I got out of the boat and rubbed pokeberries all over my face until I looked like an Indian, and then I went on. And sure enough, somewhere near Miller's Ford there was a whole party of children from Petersburg, and two men, one of 'em bein' the old fisherman Peter Oeltjen, who lived in a hut there. And they was grapplin' in the water, because someone was drownded.

" 'That was Carrie Douglas, Eliza,' " says George.

35

"Yes, that's who it was," says I. "I heard about it afterward. Well, they was so busy with this work, tryin' to get her body, that they didn't notice me on the other side of the river, and they wouldn't have knowed me anyway, with my face dyed that way. And so I got by, with only a few children callin' at me, and the men payin' no attention. But if they hadn't had enough boats of their own to row about and grapple, they would have come for me, I expect; and then I would have been caught and by this time be in the Reform School with George and Charley. Jest the same I felt sneaky about jest goin' on, for I really wanted to go over and help, because I can dive good, and I don't believe there was a man there who can swim as good as me. And because I didn't go over had lots to do with me not desertin' Miss Siddons, and bringin' her back to her home here in that wagon all the way from St. Louis.

"Well, pretty soon, I passed Miller's Ford, and I knowed it havin' been there onct with George Heigold. I knowed it by a stump near the shore and a tree that laid by the bank that grows high in one place. It's sandy and flat on one side there, and they was lots of turtles there, and on stumps and logs. And I never knowed what a river the Sangamon was before . . . not very wide, you know; but deep and ugly lookin' and full of brush and floatin' things. . . . I thought I knowed Mussel Shoals when we come to it, and Sheep's Ford, but I wasn't sure.

"Some way all this seemed like goin' to school, because it was just the same thing all the time, and not gettin' anywhere. It seemed like the Sangamon River was a thousand miles long. I knowed it emptied somewhere into the Illinois River, and that I could get to the Mississippi that way, where nobody could ever find me, and so I kept goin'. That night after Carrie Douglas was drownded I didn't know what to do about sleepin'. I thought of all the stories my pap had told me about ghosts, and how they would come back to harm people that has done 'em wrong. And I was afeard Miss Douglas' speerit would come and talk to me, just come like a mist out of the river and swoop down on me, for not helpin' get

37

her body, which I could have done so easy if I hadn't been afeard of the sheriff. Anyway, I finally rowed the boat up to the shore, and thought I'd get out and stretch, and eat standin' up, because I was that tired from settin'. It was awful still on the river and in the woods; and the terrible water was comin' down from where Miss Douglas was drownded; and I was tryin' to keep awake, and so wouldn't lie down, for fear her body might float up to the shore by me there, with her speerit over it maybe, and jest walkin' or floatin' from her body over to me, and touchin' me with cold hands. I didn't know what to do. The sun was goin' down now, too, and everythin' was gettin' stiller, except that I could hear a loaded wagon chuckin' 'way off sommers; and, of course, I was thinkin', too, that someone might see me here all alone, standin' like this and doin' nothin'; so I thought it would be better to get back in the boat and let her drift while I et my supper. I got out what I had left from what the woman had give me, and et, scoopin' up water the same as before. The bats begun to fly now, and

funny birds wheeled around and darted and
called a awful lonesome call.   And the swal-
lers was flyin' way high; and sometimes I
could hear a cow moo, or a pig squeal, so
I knowed there was people livin' sommers
near.   It was a red sunset, too, and all down
the river there was gold light, and at the
end between trees the sun, so I knowed I was
makin' west toward St. Louis.   I wanted to
go over to a house, but it was no use to think
of that; and there was nothin' ahead except
to drift and wake up sommers down the river
the same as before.   And by and by the sun
was clear down and one of the big stars
came out winkin' brighter than a fire fly,
there bein' lots of these on the river every-
wheres.   And so, I don't know when it was
I fell asleep.

"Somethin' happened here.   Maybe it was
that Cora Dunleavy changed from one foot
to the other.   Anyway, the floor creaked or
somethin', and Eliza looked around and saw
Cora standin' there by the door, her mouth
open with listenin'.   And so she said to Cora,
'Are you watchin' the corn bread, Cora?'
And, of course, Cora warn't, and as it turned

out it was burnt a little; for this was the day that Eliza had corn beef and cabbage and corn bread which George liked so much. When Eliza heard this she jumped up quick, and told me to get up and dress and so come down to dinner. And George, after hesitatin', because as he afterward told me, he was thinkin' of keepin' me upstairs all the time, until he got me safe out of the woods, told me to get up and dress, too. So I did and went downstairs, and et with the whole family. And I could see that they could hardly wait for me to finish the story. For where did Miss Siddons come in, and me bringin' her back to Petersburg?"

## CHAPTER III

"So after dinner I went on with my story and said, when I woke up the sun was jest about to come up over the river. The birds was singin', the river was sparklin', and I felt so fresh and strong, but maybe jest a little stiff, for I had layed in a kind of hollow in the boat next the seat. Anyway, I stretched out, and walked a bit, and what do you suppose? I found a good pole and a line and hook that someone had forgot and left. So I took that, and that was the third thing I took after the pie. I took it back to the boat, and begun to look around for somethin' to eat. It turned out that there was a bend in the river there, and I had stopped on this side of it; but in walkin'

41

furder down the river and so around the
bend I saw across the river a little store
and over the store the sign groceries, and
a man in front of the store sweepin', as if
he had just opened it, which was true. Now,
I took a awful chance here, for I thought
I was out of the county where I had stole
the pie, and I had heard the talk that when
you get out of the county the sheriff dasn't
arrest you from the county where you committed the crime. So I thought I'd row
across the river and see this man at the
store and help him, maybe, and so get somethin' to eat. If I had knowed that I was
still in the county, and that I was just by
Kay Watkins' farm and ferry I wouldn't
have crossed the river; and if I hadn't I don't
know how I would have et. Anyway, I
rowed over and clumb up the bank, scarin'
a big snake almost to death, and went up
to the store. It was kept by one of the
Clarys, and I saw that at first. He was red-
faced, and kind of wheezy and rollin' as he
walked, bein' fat. But his eyes was blue
and friendly, and he looked at me as if he
didn't suspect me of nothin'. I was thumpin'

42

a little in my heart, not knowin' but what he might have heard somethin' about the farmers arrestin' three boys, and me comin' so early and so funny to his store. So I was feelin' my way, and thinkin' how I'd outrun this fat man and get in my boat and row off before he could grab me. The store smelt of jeans and calico and coffee and terbacker and things; and this here Mr. Clary was walkin' around straightenin' up stacks of goods and fussin' around, at the same time chewin' somethin' makin' his jaws go from side to side, and sometimes kind of smackin' his lips a little; and I didn't know whether he was eatin' somethin' or chewin' cloves or terbacker or a piece of cinnamon. Anyway, he acted as if it was awful good; and I could feel the hot water jest gush in my mouth. He must have seed me come into the store, but if he did he didn't act that way, but jest went on with his work. Till by and by he said, 'How's the fishin', bub?' 'Fine!' says I. Then he went on to say that some fellers from near Blue Lake had come over here for catfish yesterday and had made a big haul with a sein the night

43

before, and he wondered if I had had good
luck after that. When you begin to talk
to someone and don't know what he knows
you're likely to put your foot in it if you
ain't smart. But I hadn't said where I had
my luck, so when he said this I said that
I had pretty good luck about a mile up.
He looked at me then and says, 'You're one
of the McNamaras, ain't you?' 'Yes,' says
I. 'I thought so,' says he and went right
on goin' about the store. He was the kind
of man that seems that he don't see what
is goin' on around him, and that you could
hook somethin' from easy. But I wouldn't
have hooked nothin' from him for the
world. Now I think that he had seed me
rowin' down and across the river with that
fishin' pole stickin' from the boat; but on
my part I knowed now that I was still in
Menard County from his takin' me for one
of the McNamaras; and pretty soon a man
come along and wanted some gloves which
Mr. Clary sold him; and this man was talkin'
about workin' for Kay Watkins, and about
goin' to Petersburg Saturday; so I knowed
that I had not got out of the county yet

where I took the pie. The man got the gloves and went away, and still I was there in the store; till finally Mr. Clary said that if I wasn't goin' to fish maybe I could help him clean up the back shed, which was jest through the back door of the store. I said I would; so he put me to work. I thought my stomach would twist into knots I was so hungry; but I didn't let on, but picked up all the old boxes and kindlin' and cans and things, and swept up, findin' a brand new pocket knife which had been accidentally throwed out, which I gave back to Mr. Clary, and which he took without sayin' a word, jest looked at it, and then put it back in the show-case. I expected he'd give me a cracker and a pickle for what I did for him. But finally when I got through he went to the till and fingered around a bit, then laid a nickel and a dime on the counter, without askin' me what I'd charge for the work, or anything. It was enough and I was satisfied, only it seemed so funny! Then he asked me if I liked sardines and crackers, and said he hadn't had breakfast yet, and didn't eat much anyway on account of bein'

45

fat. You see we was gettin' friendly now. So when I said I loved sardines he opened a couple of cans, and took down some crackers, and opened two bottles of brown pop, and him and me et together, him not speakin' durin' the whole time, and the water kind of runnin' out of his blue eyes. People come in to buy things and he waited on 'em, then come back and had more sardines and crackers. Finally I had all I wanted, and was full and anxious to go on down the river. I was thinkin' now pretty strong of gettin' to St. Louis, for what was the use of goin' back to Petersburg, even if I was safe? When we finished there was a half of a can of sardines left, and some crackers in the bottom of the box; so Mr. Clary told me to take 'em along and welcome; and as I started he went to the glass jar and gave me a stick of cinnamon candy, takin' some hisself and beginnin' to work his jaws as he had when I first saw him; so I knowed now what he was eatin'. I said good-by, and he didn't answer; jest kind of nodded; so I got in the boat and went on down the river, passin' Kay Watkins'

46

here than from where I stole the boat to the Illinois. I didn't know this, never havin' studied geogafy much. Say, I have forgot somethin': I know now why I didn't try for a job on the steamboat. I was afeard that if I left my rowboat to look for a job that someone might steal it; and then if I didn't get the job on the steamboat where would I be, with no rowboat and nothin'? That was it, and I forgot. There at that town, which was Beardstown, they would have stole my boat; for I had heard my pap say that Beardstown was one of the worst towns in Illinois. So on I went down the Illinois, thinkin' of Indians and of De Soto and Marquette, which we had read about in school, and lookin' at the country along the way, and gettin' food in all kinds of ways, onct gettin' a handout for helpin' some boys and men by the shore fight a bumble bee's nest, and helpin' old women as before, as I told about, and everything. And I lost track of the time and didn't know what day of the week it was, until onct I heard bells and thought it must be Sunday. And I don't know when I got to St. Louis or near

49

there; for I didn't go to the town at all. 'You didn't?' says George, 'why not?' Because I came near there at night, seein' the lights and all that, and with no place to stay; and I wanted to start out early in the mornin' lookin' for work. So I tied the boat to a snag on the shore, and after eatin' got down in the boat and fell asleep.

"The current must have pulled her loose, for when I woke up my boat had drifted, and had lodged against a house-boat on the Illinois side of the river. So I looked around me and it was a awful country: big bushes and big trees and broken-down trees, and a muddy shore, flat and awful. And pretty soon a woman come out of the house-boat and stood on the deck and spoke to me. She had a sweet voice, but you couldn't see her face for a veil which she wore. 'A veil!' says Eliza. A veil, says I. A thick white veil. And I never did see her face, except jest under it sometimes, when the wind blew or somethin' . . . then I could see more than I wanted to. You see it was Miss Siddons that I drove back here; and I never did see her face till long after this. She never took the veil off. So she stood there on the deck and spoke to me and asked me how I got there, and what I was doin', and where I was goin',' and all like that. And I made up a story to tell her, about comin' from St. Louis and a lot of things. Then she wanted to know if I wouldn't help her with some things; and I said I would, so I got out of my boat and went into the house-boat, knowin' now that if somebody stole it, I was near St. Louis anyway. When I got into the house-boat there was her husband. Then Eliza spoke up and says, 'Did her husband come back to Petersburg, too?' So then I says what would be the use of me drivin' her back if he had come?

"No, if he had come I needn't have come, and wouldn't. But we couldn't find him when we got ready to start; and I'll tell you how it was. But he was the funniest lookin' man you ever see: long hair like a woman's, and long beard, and the strangest starey eyes. And when I come in he jest looked at me without sayin' a word, jest a stiddy look. And Miss Siddons, she says to him, 'This is a boy that has come, and he

51

is goin' to help me.' I might have been afeard, because they was both so queer; but I was hungry and it looked like a chance to live and eat for a few days anyway. But there was another thing, and it was this: Miss Siddons had a nice voice that kind of went through you and made you feel safe; and I kept thinkin' that she would take off her veil pretty soon, and show me her face; and that she had the veil on after greasin' her face or somethin'. And right away she began to hum tunes, and to go about the house-boat doin' this and that; and so I set there, and watched her; and the husband jest set there, but finally got the Bible out and began to read. So seein' him read the Bible made me feel that he was a good man, and everything was all right. Then Miss Siddons asked me to get her some water, and I did; and finally we had breakfast. But Miss Siddons didn't take off the veil, and her husband set there and et without speakin', and I could see his hands, the whitest and longest fingers I ever see, with pink round nails. After breakfast Miss Siddons promised to pay me if I would stay and work, and I thought I would for a few days till I got the crooks out of my back from settin' in the boat. And besides they had pretty good food, and it was fun to watch the steamboats go up and down the river; and there was St. Louis jest across the river, which I could go to whenever I wanted. And the country back of the shore was woody and swampy and wild, with great funny birds flyin' over, big hawks and eagles, I think; and the mornin's was wonderful to get up in, and good sleeps, and, of course, no school and nothin' regular to do. An' so one thing with another I stayed on and worked for 'em.

" 'What did you do?' says George.

"Carried water, helped fish, washed dishes, run errands to a little store not far off, and helped the Master mend nets and all like that.

" 'Who was the Master?' says Eliza.

"That was what Miss Siddons made us call him. It was always the Master. But, George, I ought to go over now and see if she wants anything, for I promised I'd come to-day.

**53**

" 'Ain't you afeard of the sheriff?' says George.

"Yes, I am, says I, and that's what has made me put it off.

" 'Well', says George. 'You stay here and I'll run over and see how she is.'

"So George went out, and while he was gone, Eliza and Cora did the dishes, leavin' Joe Lester and me to talk things about the country around St. Louis, which Joe knowed when the county fairs was held there at Alton, and places like that; and where he had picked pockets, which he now told me, but sayin' to me at first to let the pie be a lesson to me, and never to get into no more trouble, and that he would tell me about jail and what it meant, and everythin'. George come back pretty soon, and said he hadn't seed Miss Siddons; but she had sent word to him by the hired girl that she was gettin' rested, and thanked him; and George sent back word to her that he would come over any time; and if there was anythin' he could do to let him know. George said he hadn't told her or the hired girl, or no one that I was with him, and so she hadn't asked after me, or why I hadn't come to see her, as I had promised. By now everybody was ready to have me go on; so George asked me now if anyone ever came to the house-boat. And I told him that people come now and then, fishermen and such; and onct in a while somebody come from some other house-boat to see Miss Siddons; but I could see from their voices, and the way they talked, that they was not ladies like her. But one day we had a visitor after I had been there about a week, which was a doctor from Alton. Before that Miss Siddons had told me that her father had been a promi-nent man and was a doctor, too—and had lived in Petersburg. So knowin' that there was a Petersburg in Virginia, I said Vir-ginia to her; and she said no, Illinois. I thought my heart would jump out of my mouth! What was this here? I had been witched or somethin' in comin' to Miss Sid-dons: and I was scared now about the sheriff and never said a word that Petersburg was my home, too, from which I had runned off. Well, then she began to talk and say that she thought it was God that had sent me

55

down the river to her, driftin' right to her, and asleep when I come. And I said maybe, hopin' that it would be good luck for me, but never sayin' a word about Illinois. So she told me about her father bein' rich onct, and about her bein' a girl and havin' everythin' and now comin' to this; and it made me wonder. She'd say this when the Master was away. And she told me almost at first that her father had a friend in Alton, a fine doctor, and that she had writ him a letter to come and see her, and give her somethin' to get well, and that he had writ to her that he would come sometime. And so one day when the Master was off sommers, because he did wander off by hisself a lot, this here doctor came. He must have been in St. Louis, but anyway he came in a little boat, and I saw him sightin' around. I was on the deck and saw him, and he hollered and asked where the Siddons house-boat was, for there was others there, you see; and I says this is it. Jest then Miss Siddons come to the door, and says what is it, and then the doctor come close. She knew him and says, 'This is me, Doctor Fenton, this is Julia

Seward'; and there she stood with this heavy white veil over her face so that her own father would not have knowed her if it had been him. So the doctor got out of the launch and came into the house-boat, and I stayed near outside to help if anything was wanted but also to hear what was said. I couldn't see, just hear. And Miss Siddons says to the doctor, 'I want you to look at my face,' and so I guess he looked at it, for he says, 'Um,' and began to ask her questions, and I heard her tell him that she was gettin' wrinkles, and didn't want 'em on account of her stage work, and that she went to somebody and had wax put under the skin, to take the wrinkles out, and so her face got this way, all splotched and sore, and that's why she wore the white veil. And the doctor told her he could do nothin', that she would have to go to a hospittle, and have the skin cut, and growed new again, and that it would take time and would hurt; and would cost some money, too, unless she could come to Alton where he would do his best for her, by gettin' a doctor there who did such things to do it as cheap as he could.

57

And then the doctor asked about Miss Siddons' mother, and about how long her father had been dead, and about their old times together when they was boys in Chandlerville before old Mr. Seward moved to Petersburg or was married or anythin'. Then he come out to get in his boat and go away. And Miss Siddons come to the door, and said good-by in a sad voice and he went; and she begun to sing after she got back in the house-boat, to sing that song.

" 'Sing what, Kit?' says George.

"Why, 'When Other Lips and Other Hearts' . . . and in the saddest voice you ever heard, and I was about to cry I was so lonesome and sorry for her. It was a hot afternoon, the sky dusty and sick, and the water had bad smells and the big birds was flyin'. And so I set there wishin' I was dead or somethin', and pretty soon she come to me and asked me where the Master was. 'Where's the Master, Conrad?' I had give my name to her as Conrad, and so she called me that. I didn't know where he was. And then she began to show me things, it was now that she started that. You see in the

58

house-boat there was two bunks, one for
her and one for him; and I slept on top of a
big chest that was in the corner, which she
put blankets and things on, and then they
was folded up in the day, and she put a
drape on it and made it look nice like a
bureau or somethin.' Well, after the doctor
had went she asked me to lift up the top
of this chest, and I did, and saw the most
wonderful things I ever saw. Like circus
things so fine and all covered with gold and
things, and besides lots of pitchers. But
I didn't see very well what they was. And
Miss Siddons made me hold the top till she
got some things out of the chest, after havin'
unlocked it with a key which she carried
in her dress. Then she went to the winder
and looked, and come back to me and said:
'I'll show you some things when I was a
girl,' and so she showed me photographs.
First one of a beautiful girl in a cap, with
curls, and wearin' a wonderful tight nice
dress, a skatin' costume it was, and she was
on her skates. And Miss Siddons says,
'That's me when I was fourteen and was
the champion skater; that's me,' and I felt

59

the veil move as her words said this. It was
awful funny and scarey. And then she
showed me other pitchers when she was eight-
een, all in fine dresses and when she was on
the stage. 'I was happy then and had
money,' she said . . . and so it went, and
she was goin' to go right on showin' me
the things in the chest. But she heard
somethin', she did, but I didn't hear nothin';
her ears was keener than mine. And so she
hopped up and looked out of the winder and
says, 'The Master is comin';' and she put
the things in the chest, and locked it; and
by the time the Master come, she was at
the stove pretendin' to cook. So the Master
come in and set down and began to read the
Bible. He was always readin' the Bible, and
he claimed he could be a prophet and tell
what was goin' to happen.

" 'Did he know that the doctor from Alton
had been there?' says Ernest. 'Did he
prophesy about that?'

"I don't know, says I. He didn't say
nothin' about it, and she didn't. And, of
course, I didn't. I never told nothin' to
either one of them. I let them tell me things,

God told him that he was to be punished that way, and to have the care of her for life, on account of the sins he had committed when he was young and rich and fine to look at, and besides to make himself love her was part of the punishment; and to be patient with her and take care of her when he could hardly stand to do it was part of his punishment; and his joy, because it was his salvation; though he could hardly stand sometimes to be near her; an' that he was goin' to stay by her until the time come for him to be crucified, and go to his Father.

"He talked so earnest that I was scared, and it took all the afternoon for him to tell me this, and lots more, maybe, that I have forgot. So we went back to the house-boat; and it was about evenin', and when we come into the house-boat it was all still, and the Master begun to call to Miss Siddons; and it turned out that she was lyin' down, and maybe cryin', on account of what the doctor had told her. The Master called to her again, and she kind of turned on the bunk; it was awful hot in there at sundown, and of course considerable flies and bugs, and the smell of

65

the river; and Miss Siddons asked him what he wanted and he said, 'Are you sleepin'? Watch and pray. You know what the Bible says.' 'Yes,' says Miss Siddons, in a kind of dead voice, 'I know what it says, and you will never understand me. I would never be here if I had not watched and prayed.' 'For what?' says he. She didn't answer him. And he went on: 'You have watched and prayed for the glory of the world, for beauty, as you call it, and God has give you that face for it.' The Master would be cross sometimes, and then his voice was awful to hear and cut right through you with a cut like a knife; and when he said this I could see that she was cut. She turned in the bunk, like you see a worm sometimes when you cut it with a knife. And the Master set down and began to read the Bible, and I felt so bad I went out and set on the deck and looked at the sun goin' down, and watched a steamboat pass, and wondered if I hadn't better run off to-night, and get out of this.

" 'What made you stay?' says George.

" 'On account of her,' says I; I was so sorry for her. I didn't care for him or what become of him, but I was sorry for her, so that I was about to cry lots of times; but also, as I said before, I had gone past that place on the Sangamon River where Miss Carrie Douglas was drownded and didn't do nothin' on account of bein' afraid of bein' caught; and now I had no reason to leave Miss Siddons, except jest the way it made me feel, nothin' to fear of the sheriffs or anything. And for the same reason I come back with her and took a chance of gettin' arrested just because I couldn't leave her in the lurch. And I'll go to the reform school now if I have to with George and Charley.

" 'Maybe the Master's talks about the truth and the Bible have had something to do with your resolutions, Kit?" says Ernest.

" 'No,' says I. That man couldn't make me believe nothin'. I know he was crazy. For that night after we had been fishin', and after Miss Siddons had got the supper and we had gone to bed, it must have been in the middle of the night, and I felt Miss Siddons shakin' me and callin' me to get up and go for the Master. 'Where is he?' says I. 'He's in the river,' says she. And so we hurried

out, and there he was up to his neck wadin'
toward us. He had tried to walk on the
water and went under, on account of not
havin' enough faith, he said, and because he
had been cross with Miss Siddons the afternoon before when we come back, as I have
told. So we pulled him ashore and got dry
things on him, and then he prayed, and Miss
Siddons just sighed and turned on her bunk.
The next mornin' I had to hitch up the horse
and drive the Master down to the store to
get some things. And on the way down the
Master said that he was walkin' all right and
could have got across the river to St. Louis
if he hadn't started to think about bein'
cross to Miss Siddons the afternoon before;
that the devil made him think of that, and
when he did he began to sink; and he wondered what Peter thought of when he sank;
for accordin' to the Bible he was walkin' all
right, and then suddenly went down. And
he said the devil always did that, and always
got the best of people by makin' 'em think
of somethin' bad when they was doin' all
right; and in that way the power of God was
took away from 'em.

68

Joe, that nobody knowed who did it; but that
he knowed that Joe had nothin' to do with it,
because at ten o'clock Joe was with him at his
house; and he asked the judge to swear him
and Ernest too who was along. 'To what
point?' asked Mr. Sprinkle, the state's attorney, speakin' awful keen. And George said
to the point that Joe was with him at ten
o'clock and couldn't be at Mr. Tallman's
store at the same time.

" 'Who all was at your house last night?'
asked the state's attorney.

"So George said he thought for sure that
Mr. Sprinkle had got him and knew that I
was hidin' in George's house. And he said
Mr. Sprinkle's thin lips grew thinner, and his
forehead narrower, and his jaw set more, and
his voice sounded more like a file on a whet-
stone. George was scared, but he went on
to tell Mr. Sprinkle everybody that was at
the house except me; and the state's attorney
didn't take it up, and so George seed that
he didn't know about me. Then Mr. Sprinkle
in a high-falutin' way asked the witnesses
to be sworn. That was done and George and
Ernest swore that Joe was at George's house

till past ten o'clock, where Joe lived anyway. Then the state's attorney cross-questioned 'em, but got nothin', George said.
Then Joe wanted to be sworn, though the
judge told him he could stand on his right
and not testify, but Joe wanted to anyway,
for he had been in court lots, and knew his
rights anyway. So Joe got on the stand and
told his story clear. And finally they swore
Mr. Tallman's son who wasn't sure it was Joe
after all, and got tangled when George asked
him some questions. And finally the judge
said as Mr. Tallman's son didn't see the faces
of the men and wasn't really sure, and because George and Ernest was so sure he
wouldn't issue no warrant, because no jury
would ever convict anyway, and there was
nothin' to it so fur as Joe was concerned;
and so told Joe to go home. Mr. Sprinkle
was mad, George said, and didn't want to
talk with George, who thought it was a good
time to talk about George and Charley in
the Reformatory who had stole the pie, and
about me. Sprinkle smiled kind of sick,
George said, and said to George, 'Well,
George, I suppose you will soon be at work

tryin' to get those young burglars out of the Reformatory that we sent up while you was in California. There's some talk here among some of your kind of people that there was a injustice done them boys. But I want to tell you now that you will have your hands full.'

" 'You are talkin' about the boys that stole that pie?' says George.

" 'Yes,' says Mr. Sprinkle, 'about the boys that stole the pie, and broke into a store the night before and stole terbacker and cigarettes which we found on 'em; and who would have tooken everything in that farmer's house if they had not been caught before they did it; and who broke all the chairs and furniture in jail; and who was the cause of the death of Mitch Miller by leadin' him into bad ways, and some more things, if I wanted to talk about it, which I don't. The O'Brien boy will be back some day, when he gets tired of wanderin', and then the law will take care of him, the same as it will everybody else who violates the law while I am state's attorney; and the criminals around here will find out that they hain't got a good-natured man like

75

Hardy Kirby to deal with, who used to let people off. By and by criminals around here will see that this is a civilized community, and that the law must be respected.' And then he went on to Joe Lester and he said that Joe's parole was hangin' by a slender thread, and that one of these days he would grab up Joe and have him sent back to the penitentiary where he belongs.

"So George said he was good-natured with Mr. Sprinkle, desirin' to keep him from gettin' madder, and maybe comin' after Joe or somethin'. And that Mr. Sprinkle just turned on his heel and walked off without sayin' good-day or anythin'; and so George and Joe and Ernest had come back.

"Well, I could see that George was bothered some about what they would do with me; and he said that he had wrote a letter downtown to get a report of the Reformatory to see what kind of boys went there, if they was boys there that had done somethin' besides doin' some little thing like stealin' a pie; and what kind of boys went there as to religion and the like, and parents and homes, and all that; and he said that he had asked his lawyer to get up papers to have George Heigold and Charley King pardoned. But as to what he was goin' to do to keep me from fallin' into the hands of Mr. Sprinkle he didn't say, or seem to know. Meantime he and all the rest wanted to hear the end of my story; and so after supper, we got in a good place upstairs, and I began again, with Cora and Joe and everybody listenin'. I had left off where the Master tried to walk to St. Louis on the Mississippi River, and so I took it up there, sayin' that the next day after this, the Master wandered away early and that give me and Miss Siddons a chance for a long talk. I helped her with the work, and took care of the horse and everything. And then she got out her key and opened up the chest and begun to show me things. She showed me lots of pitchers of herself, great big pitchers like Burr Robbins used to have here for the circus; and photographs showin' her in all kinds of fine dresses, and pitchers of fine gentlemen and ladies, all dressed in wonderful clothes, and which she said was great actors and actresses that she knowed. And she showed me lots of newspaper pieces

77

about herself, and where she had been and
what she had done. For onct she was in
London and sung before the Prince of Wales
and a big crowd, and even the queen was
comin', only she was sick or her husband was
sick and couldn't.

"This seemed to remind Eliza of what she
knowed her own self about Miss Siddons.
For Eliza now said that onct there was a
woman livin' in Petersburg named Eva Hor-
ace, who was a friend of Miss Siddons, and
always stood by her through thick and thin;
and that this here Eva sent the word around
to tease the people here who never believed
that Miss Siddons amounted to nothin', that
Miss Siddons was havin' all this wonderful
time in London before the Prince of Wales,
provin' it by a letter from Miss Siddons,
which Eva showed to everybody, jest to
tease 'em. And Eliza said that the song
which Miss Siddons had sung before the
Prince was 'When Other Lips and Other
Hearts.' So I said I'd bet it was, because I
had heard her sing it on the house-boat down
the Mississippi. Then George said that onct
he was in Chicago, and Miss Siddons' pitcher

78

was on the walls and billboards all over the town; and she was at the head of some kind of a company and pretty near the top. This reminded Eliza of something which was that at the same time that George was in Chicago some other people from Petersburg was there and come back sayin' that Miss Siddons couldn't act at all, and that her face had grown so hard that even from the stage it looked like it had been varnished and then caked. Then Eliza said that Mr. Seward, one of the finest men ever in Petersburg, had broke his heart over Julia, on account of her marriages or somethin' like that; and that she called it a poor return to him for all that he done for her, not to say a poor return to herself for this art business, as they call it. And that it proved that the way of stayin' in your place and doin' your duty was the only way that pays. And that Miss Siddons should be thankful to God that her mother had stuck by her all these years, and had received her back home sick and ruined, and with a face that she wouldn't show to the town. Eliza had been over to the Seward house and had seen old Mrs. Seward; and she said that old Mrs. Seward spoke of Miss Siddons just like she was a little girl yet, instead of bein' almost a old woman herself. Then George spoke up and said he knew Dr. Walcott over in Springfield and knew him well, and that he was goin' to get him to come over and see Miss Siddons and see what he could do for her face. After all this they wanted me to go on with my story; so I did.

"Well, Miss Siddons showed me all these things. And she had a dress in the bottom of her chest which she said she had wore when she was in London or New York, I forget which. It was all of silk and braid and was wonderful. And she showed me some laces and ribbons and a lot of fans, with spangles like the dresses of circus ladies, and some with painted pitchers on 'em; and it was so funny seein' these things there on the house-boat, and hearin' her talk with no other sound but the cry of a water bird, or maybe the whistle of a enjine over in St. Louis or some-thin' like that. It took her a long time to show me everything, because she had to tell me what they was as she showed 'em; and there was always the danger of the Master

comin' back and catchin' us. Till at last one
day she reached way down in the bottom of
the chest and brung out a bundle of hand-
kerchiefs and unwrapped 'em, and there was
a velvet case; and she opened that and there
was the most beautiful green ring you ever
see, which she said was a emerald and worth
lots of money, enough to buy a lot to bury
her in, and give her a fine stone and everythin' when she died. And she said she would
never part with it until she could get money
no other way. She made me promise never
to tell the Master that she had the ring,
which I did, and kept too. And onct in a
while she would get awful tired and maybe
cry a little, and sometimes she would have to
put on a fresh veil, because it was so hot.
She had lots of these here veils, which she
washed and kept herself in a pile near the
stove. She told me about bein' in China and
Japan, and San Francisco, besides all over
Europe; and she had pitcher cards of all
these places and sometimes a pitcher of herself and someone, sometimes a man standin'
near some funny big building or church or
somethin', or a mountain or a river. I could

hardly wait for her to show me all she had,
and it took lots of time from day to day when
the Master was away prayin' or settin' in
what he called his garden, which was a clump
of bushes and weeds down the river, a awful
hot place and looked like snakes would be
thick there. And she was always on the
watch for fear he would come back and catch
her goin' through this chest. Onct she
thought she heard him, and she closed it
quick and looked out of the winder. He
wasn't there, and she said, 'I don't want him
to know what's in here, Conrad, for the truth
is he married me for my money. He thought
I had enough for him to rest up on. He was
played out too, havin' been a actor hisself.
And he thought I could support him, which
I couldn't without sellin' my things in this
chest, which I won't do.'

" 'Did she ever say why she married him?'"
George asked me.

" 'No more,' I said, 'than to hint that she
was alone, and had a hard time to get anyone to do anythin' for her, on account of
bein' sick, her face you know and everything.'

" 'Did she say this was her third husband?' asked George.

" 'I took it that way,' says I.

" 'Who was her second husband, do you know?'

"Well, she talked a lot about a man she met in San Francisco, I said, after she come back from China. She had gone over there with her company or somethin' and things went bad, so she come back to America, come to San Francisco. And then she would talk about this man and what a wonderful time they had, and what a fine house they had there and about the flowers in the garden and the birds, and what wonderful times they had drivin' about the city of San Francisco, and out by the sea and everythin'; for she said this man had wonderful horses and was rich to all appearances but wasn't really; and then she was expectin' to make lots of money, and expected to be the most wonderful actress in the world. Miss Siddons said that this here man claimed to be the son of a duke or somethin' in England, and would be a duke or somethin' some day hisself, and wanted her to marry him and be a duchess.

And when she was tellin' me this the flies
would be buzzin' there in the house-boat, and
the river smellin', and everythin' lonesome
like I told. And she would say, 'Yes a
duchess, and look at me now! Jest look at
me!' Then her veil would trimble, and I
would be wishin' that I was back in Petersburg, and had never had nothin' to do with
that pie. So Miss Siddons said that this
man after quite a while said he was
goin' to Canada to work, and told her that
the money he had made on the races was gone,
and he would have to go to work on some
of the land that belonged to the duke, his
father. So they quit friendly, and how they
was divorced, she never said and I don't
know. Then she said she got money again
which she had spent or lost in China, and
decided to go to England. And it was this
time that she sang before the Prince of
Wales that song, 'When Other Lips and
Other Hearts.' But what was most wonderful, she said that one day, one night it was,
she got a card from this man when she was
actin' in London which had a duke for a
father, the card bein' brought to her after

84

the show, and that he wanted to see her.
So she saw him and they had supper and
talked, and he wanted her to come up to his
place in the country and visit him for over
Sunday.  So she said she went, and that it
was the most wonderful castle you ever saw
and the most wonderful grounds around it.
She had a pitcher of it too, which she showed
me out of her trunk while tellin' me this.
You see the duke had died, and this here man
was now the duke hisself, and she showed me
a pitcher of him too, sayin' there was quite
a difference between livin' in a castle and
livin' in a house-boat, and quite a difference
between bein' a duchess and bein' the wife
of the Master, which she said with a laugh
and then a sigh.  Well, she said, she went
into the castle and was taken to the most
lovely rooms, and had maids give her to wait
on her and everythin'; and finally when it
was dinner time, she went down to the parlor,
and there was the duke to meet her besides
the duke's sister and the duchess, for the duke
had married; and so they must have been
divorced or somethin' or he couldn't have
done it.  It was all wonderful, Miss Siddons

85

said, a fine dinner and wonderful, an
duke as nice as could be and the du
friendly, too, who I guess didn't know n
about Miss Siddons and the duke bein
ried onct before in San Francisco.
Miss Siddons showed me a pitcher o
self, taken the next day after this dinne
the duke and the duchess, and she wa
beautiful, I believe the most beautiful v
I ever saw, and I don't wonder the d
liked her. Well, she said, that aft
dinner they went walkin' in the flowe
den; and there was other men, prin
somethin' there, and they walked wi
duchess and the duke's sister, and the
walked with Miss Siddons. So then th
told her that after he went to Canad
he hadn't worked long before his fathe
and that he became the duke hisse l
had money and so went to England _
then Miss Siddons mentioned someth
hadn't before, which was that she had
duke money, or sent him money after
to Canada; and that while her and th
was walkin' in the garden together
rest of the company was on ahe

86

the show, and that he wanted to see her.
So she saw him and they had supper and
talked, and he wanted her to come up to his
place in the country and visit him for over
Sunday. So she said she went, and that it
was the most wonderful castle you ever saw
and the most wonderful grounds around it.
She had a pitcher of it too, which she showed
me out of her trunk while tellin' me this.
You see the duke had died, and this here man
was now the duke hisself, and she showed me
a pitcher of him too, sayin' there was quite
a difference between livin' in a castle and
livin' in a house-boat, and quite a difference
between bein' a duchess and bein' the wife
of the Master, which she said with a laugh
and then a sigh. Well, she said, she went
into the castle and was taken to the most
lovely rooms, and had maids give her to wait
on her and everythin'; and finally when it
was dinner time, she went down to the parlor,
and there was the duke to meet her besides
the duke's sister and the duchess, for the duke
had married; and so they must have been
divorced or somethin' or he couldn't have
done it. It was all wonderful, Miss Siddons
85

said, a fine dinner and wonderful, and the duke as nice as could be and the duchess friendly, too, who I guess didn't know nothin' about Miss Siddons and the duke bein' married onct before in San Francisco. Then Miss Siddons showed me a pitcher of herself, taken the next day after this dinner with the duke and the duchess, and she was that beautiful, I believe the most beautiful woman I ever saw, and I don't wonder the duchess liked her. Well, she said, that after the dinner they went walkin' in the flower garden; and there was other men, princes or somethin' there, and they walked with the duchess and the duke's sister, and the duke walked with Miss Siddons. So then the duke told her that after he went to Canada that he hadn't worked long before his father died, and that he became the duke hisself, and had money and so went to England. And then Miss Siddons mentioned somethin' she hadn't before, which was that she had give the duke money, or sent him money after he got to Canada; and that while her and the duke was walkin' in the garden together and the rest of the company was on ahead and

86

couldn't hear, the duke said that he would
always be her friend for helpin' him out
when he was in Canada. Then when it come
Monday she went back to London again and
to actin'. She showed me letters that the
duke had wrote her, all with crowns on 'em
and unicorns, she said they was, and writin'
in Latin; but I didn't read the letters. I
only saw that he called her 'goddess,' and
sweet words like that. So it went day by
day. I was takin' care of the horse, runnin'
errands, helpin' her about the house-boat;
and she was tired all the time and sighin',
and I had to help cook, and allus washed
the dishes; and finally I was tryin' to get
away and go to St. Louis, for what was there
to this? But she would jest beg me to stay,
to stay anyway till she could get to the doctor
and get her face cured. And it was so hot
there by the river you could hardly live.
Onct when I went in swimmin' I was almost
scalt. The water was yellow and dirty, too,
and so I just seemed to be gettin' my dues
for that pie, to be there with such people
and to have it tougher than in jail. The
Master was cross sometimes, and as the

weather got hotter and sicker he seemed to
get crosser and crazier. He would get up of
a mornin' and go to the river and wash his
face and hands and come back with his hair
all wet and slicked back and his eyes bright
and lookin' around quick, or sometimes slow
as if he didn't know where he was. And
sometimes he would say, 'Where are we?
How do we happen to be here? Is this me,
I wonder?' And when we had breakfast or
before, he would throw back his head and say
a prayer that would jest send the shivers
down your back and fetch the tears out of
your eyes. I couldn't help from cryin' sometimes. And there Miss Siddons would set
with that veil on, and you couldn't see her
eyes how they looked nor what she was thinkin'. It was like havin' a corpse at the table
when this was goin' on. Sometimes the Master would get up from breakfast and lift his
hands to the ceilin' and almost yell words,
such as, 'My God, why hast Thou forsaken
me!' or onct, 'God in heaven, think of it we
had bacon this morning.' For that was the
time when we did have extra good bacon from
some fishermen who had give it to me when

they broke camp, for me havin' helped them with their boats and such like.

"The Master had a sword which he said he used when actin'. And sometimes he would take this sword down and jab with it, sayin', 'Ha, varlet!' or 'Have at you!' and other words like poetry in the Fourth Reader. And onct Miss Siddons kind of laughed from behind her veil when he was doin' this. I looked at her and saw the veil trimblin' like a curtain that the wind blows, and saw that she was really laughin' hearty; and she said: 'What a pair we are. I can laugh at it when it don't hurt too much.' And the Master looked at her and a awful look come into his eyes as if he thought she was mockin' him and had no right to, that he was still a big man, and maybe bigger than ever. You see he could have run her with the sword and me too, and done it when we was asleep; and sometimes I was afeard he would. I would make up my mind I wouldn't go to sleep, so I could watch him, and then before I knowed it I was asleep, and the next mornin' I was alive.

"Well, I couldn't understand either one of them. Their stories didn't jibe. Sometimes

89

he would say he married her for money, to
be paid for takin' care of her, but what he
did I never could see, except jest to be with
her; and after I come I could see that she
was glad to have jest me, and have him away
whenever he wanted to go. Sometimes he
would say that he married her because God
told him to, and that he was servin' God in
watchin' over her. But all the while I could
see that money come from her, except jest
the dribs he'd get onct in a while for a fish.
But where she had her money I never knowed
and I don't believe the Master knowed. She
would take it out of her pocket always; yet
we was all livin' cheap there on the river
like that. But when she got out of money
in her pocket, and had to get some more
from sommers, I don't know where she got
it. Maybe it was from the chest; maybe
from a hole in the ground out in the jungle
where sometimes she went when the Master
was away, sayin' that she would take a walk.

"Well, one day she was showin' me things
in the chest. It was in the afternoon, and
this was only a week last Monday. She was
showin' me things and tellin' me what a won-

derful life she had had after all, and that she
didn't regret nothin'; that she had seed everythin' in the world, and had riches and
people to like her and all that; and that
everythin' went in a lifetime, and that she
was goin' to get her face cured if she could,
which she had really neglected, owin' to bein'
sick, and comin' up the river, and on account of the Master and everythin', and
that she was goin' to get hold of some kind
of new life, she didn't know what; and she
made me promise to stick by her, and that
she would make it worth while; and she was
talkin' cautious about the Master, but I could
sort of feel that she wanted to get away from
him, or have him get away from her. This
was when the Master had gone to his garden
to pray and read the Bible. He had been
sayin' for days that it would soon be time
to go to St. Louis and be killed and go to
heaven. When he talked this way she jest
set there with her face turned toward him,
but you couldn't see what she thought on account of the veil; but sometimes it would puff
out a little, and then I knowed she was
breathin' harder; but whether she cried or

91

tried to keep from laughin' I don't know. I know I was scared and lonesome. So as I said he was away in his garden, and we thought we was alone and was not thinkin' about him. When suddenly he sneaked in on us before we had time to shut the chest; and he run over to it with kind of a growl, and kept her from shuttin' it. He took hold of the lid, and when she fought him back he pushed her to one side, and she kind of fell over, and her veil got twisted and I saw her face a little. I almost wanted to die when I saw her face! And I was mad and madder; so I took hold of the Master, and he flung me off as if I was a straw. I thought I was strong; but he had the strongest arms I ever see. So she set there cryin' and beggin' him to quit; and I took a hand and told him it warn't fair for him to go into her things. But he paid no attention to me or to her, jest went on clawin' things out of the chest, the pitchers, dresses and everythin' and throwin' the pitchers and photographs and newspapers and letters and dresses all over the floor. She sank kind of down, and cried, and wrung her hands, and kept beggin' the Master to stop. Her veil

92

got twisted a little on her face again; but I couldn't see much; and the Master was talkin' and ravin' about sin, and about the vanity of fine clothes, and everythin' like that; and sayin' that salvation was the only thing, and God was patient but would sometime get mad and punish people. So he was goin' through this chest, and ravin' about Babylon and the curses of God, and actin' jest as crazy as he could. All the time she was beggin' him to leave her things alone, and she asked me to stop him, which I couldn't, as he was awful strong, and really now gettin' madder and more dangerous all the time.

"Well, at last the worst happened, jest as Miss Siddons feared, I guess. He got down to the bottom of the chest, and found the velvet case with the emerald ring in it. He opened it, and looked. Then he raised his eyes to see her, then he looked at me, then at the ring, and he rolled his eyes and sighed like; and his chest kind of heaved, his hair stood up, his beard trimbled, his long white fingers shook. And so he stood there. And Miss Siddons begun to cry, whimper like, and to beg him to put the ring down and

93

go away. But he paid no attention. He jest stood there, trimblin' all over, and finally he said, 'So this is it, this is what has been the matter! This is the sin that has been in this house all the time, chokin' me to death. This is what kept me from faith and made me sink in the river, and kept the angels away from me who want to come and take care of me, and give me faith. This is the snake's eye, the scale of the dragon, this vanity from the evil days of the world, this price of goodness and salvation.' And so he raved on and finally began to walk the floor.

"I was watchin' him now pretty close, and I saw him put his hand in his pocket, and then take it out and look at the ring, and hold it away from him and say, 'beautiful damnation,' or somethin' like that. And then Miss Siddons seemed to get hold of herself, and she took after the Master to get the ring. She clawed at him and tussled with him, but finally he pushed her off, and grabbed up his sword, and went over to the winder, and stood lookin' toward St. Louis.

"It was toward evening, and the sun looked
94

hot and dusty as a tramp on a July evenin';
and a awful loneliness was over the whole
place. The flies was buzzin' lonesome in the
room, and the crows was flyin' and callin'
over the terrible woods near the shore; and
I was scared and sick. I made up my mind
to run away this night and get out of this.
I couldn't stand no more. And there stood
the Master, with his sword in one hand, lookin' out of the winder as if he was thinkin',
and havin' the ring in his other hand and
finally takin' it up to his eyes, which I could
see and lookin' at it; and finally he walked
to the winder, and jest throwed the ring out
as fur as he could. I came over quick then
and saw jest a little flip of the water about
a hundred feet from the house. And so the
ring was sunk in the Mississippi! Then Miss
Siddons screamed and said, 'You talk about
crucifixion . . . what of me?' and she kind
of keeled over. Then he stood in the middle
of the room, calm like, and began to say in a
low draggin' voice, 'My time is come.' And
he turned quick and walked out of the room,
with his head bent down to his breast, and
his hands folded in front of him. I looked

out of the other winder, and saw him walk
away into the woods and disappear. Then I
undressed and swum out to where I seed the
ring fall, and dived for the ring, and dived
and dived, as long as I could stand it. But
the bottom was nothin' but mud, and I
couldn't find a thing. I swum back to the
house-boat pretty tired. And there was Miss
Siddons. She wanted to know what I was
doin' and I told her, and she jest said that
I was too good. Then she wanted to know
where the Master went, and I told her. And
she went back into the house-boat cryin'.

"I got the supper, and we waited for the
Master, but he didn't come. It got night,
and I offered to take her for a row on the
river, but she wouldn't go, but jest set there
still and thinkin'. Then I went out and dived
some more, but it was no use, and I jest did
it thinkin' there might be a chance. Finally
after I was dressed again I set on the deck
with the water slappin' the green stuff near
the shore, and the bats flyin' and these here
night birds flyin' and cryin'. And after a
while I was clear tired and sleepy from all
that divin' and everythin', so I went in and

went to bed; but Miss Siddons was not asleep.

"You see I couldn't leave her. If this ring business hadn't happened I was goin' this night. But now that it had and the Master was gone, I couldn't leave her. All the same I was afeard he might return durin' the night and kill us both, and I thought maybe before he did I might hit him with the poker or somethin' and so save us. So I fell asleep while really tryin' to stay awake and watch for him. I slept and dreamed of him and the sword. By and by it was day. Miss Siddons got up sayin' that she hadn't slept at all, and she wished she was me; that I slept like the dead. And so we got breakfast and I helped her and with the dishes. She was cryin' a little sometimes; and finally she said she would wait till night and if he didn't come back she would do somethin'. She said now for the first that her mother had a good house in Petersburg, and as mean as the town had been for her, it was her home and she had no other, and maybe it was time to go home and die. She made me feel awful for her. So in the afternoon she had me get things ready. There was the chest to put her

97

things in again; and she wanted to take the chickens, and her little dog. Lots of things she had to leave, because we couldn't carry everythin' in the wagon, but she said it didn't matter much. She wanted me to drive her to Petersburg, and she would give me a fine reward and then she would let me go to do whatever I wanted to.

"So what was I goin' to do? If I come back to Petersburg there was the sheriff, and if I left her and went over to St. Louis and got work, what would become of her? All this I was thinkin' after I had got everything ready to start; and I was settin' on the deck of the house-boat lookin' over at St. Louis, and wonderin' what it was like if I could get there, and maybe there was work there for me, and a chance to get up in the world; and here on account of that pie, and really jest on account of tryin' to make somethin' of myself, and get to a place where there was work and a chance I was in this trouble and caught between goin' back and bein' arrested, or runnin' away from Miss Siddons, who had nobody but me and needed me so bad. What can a person do in such a fix as that? All

the time Miss Siddons was indoors lyin' on
the couch and sayin' nothin'; and there we
was, not knowin' but what the Master would
come back and keep us from goin' and me
from takin' her even if I wanted to. It
might be that the sheriff and Mr. Sprinkle
was here enforcin' the law and doin' their
duty; but there I was sufferin' everything,
and tryin' to decide what I should do. And
it seemed if I did my duty by bringin' her
back to her old home it would only help them
to do theirn by arrestin' me. So it was night
after while, and I got somethin' for her to
eat, and brought it to her, and she called
me a treasure, and begged me again not to
leave her. She wanted to start right off; but
she said that she didn't feel well enough, and
she was sure the Master was gone for good.
I was afeard she might die; and what would
I do then? And now I remembered a story
I had read in the Reader at school, where a
good dog got shot because he was found with
some sheep killin' dogs, but had done nothin'
hisself. Which wasn't me, because I had stole
the pie as much as George and Charley;
but maybe I was to be kilt too, because they

had got me started, just as Mitch Miller was got into flippin' cars and so was kilt, even if he was knocked under by the brakeman. For it warn't George and Charley theirselves but what comes from bein' with 'em that made the trouble, for me and for Mitch. Maybe one thing was goin' to lead to another until the Master would come back this night and kill me, as well as Miss Siddons.

"The sun was settin' finally, and I could see a star in the red of the sky in the west and I could see the smoke and the buildin's of St. Louis, and the river was still, only one steamboat on her, and a few fishermen way down by the lonesome woods. Suddenly Miss Siddons was standin' on the deck before I knew it. And I was settin' there, and she stood there before doin' anything; and then all at once she raised her hands up to the sky as if she was about to pray. She was facin' St. Louis, lookin' toward St. Louis, and with her hands up to the sky. She didn't have no hat on, just the veil like she allus had. And slow like she took off the veil . . . yes, jest took it right off, and stood their facin' St. Louis. Then I saw her face! And

100

I never seed anything so terrible. Now I must say somethin' here to show how I felt. Onct there was a show here in Petersburg which I went to, which had a devil in it, and I never could forget it. This devil had red lines, red as blood, between his eyebrows on his forehead; and red lines under his eyes, and red lines on his cheeks runnin' down to the corners of his mouth, jest as red as blood, or maybe as red as red paint. And this here devil scart all of us. Well, that is the way Miss Siddons looked when she took off her veil; she had two red lines between her eyebrows, and red lines under her eyes, and red lines runnin' down to the corners of her mouth, jest as red as blood or red paint; except that I could see there in that light shinin' on her face that the red was not paint but was inflammations, which had broke at the edges and looked crusty and raw like a cherry pie which has broke at the edge. Well, there she was lookin' toward St. Louis! There she was with her veil off! And her hands lifted to that sky with sad birds wheelin' in it and the bats flyin'! And she began to sing. Gee whiz! but my back jest

101

shivered. I jest set there with my back shiverin', not able to do a thing, to ask her a thing; and the tears runnin' out of my eyes. And she was singin' and jest makin' the woods and the river stagger with the sound of her voice, which was almost the strongest I ever heard. And singin' that song.

" 'What song?' says Ernest.

" 'When Other Lips and Other Hearts,' says I. And she sang it so you could hear it way down the river, and back into the woods, which echoed back 'you'll remember me,' as if someone was sayin' they'd remember; and her voice went way up to the sky. Anybody on the river for a mile could have heard her; only there weren't no one but them fishermen and me.

"So I began to cry for thinkin' of this while tellin' George and Eliza and the rest about it; and Eliza come over to me and kissed me jest like I've seed mothers kiss their boys when they was hurt or somethin'. And I cried when she was singin' too, you bet I cried. It was so lonesome and I was so sorry for her. Her voice went up and down the river and seemed to die off in them awful woods and jungles way back of the house-boat; and the Mississippi jest went crawlin' on as if it didn't care, and the night birds went wheelin' as if they didn't care for nothin' except the bugs they was chasin'; and when she came to the words, 'Then you'll remember me,' she put all her power into it, so that the woods jest reeled like a drunk man with the sound; and of course anyone could see that nobody remembered her, and that's maybe why she sang and sang so piti-ful. So I set there scared and cryin', and finally when she had sang the last words, she come over to me and put her hand on my head and said, 'Stay by me, Conrad, till I get home.' Well, if I was to go to twenty jails or be hung I would have stayed by her. I was so sorry for her that if I had knowed that when I drove into Petersburg the sheriff would be waitin' there in the Rock Creek road, all ready to grab me I would have promised and would have brought her back to her mother. So I promised her. Says I, 'I will stick by you, Miss Siddons, till I rot.' And then she bust out cryin' and says, 'You don't know who you are, Conrad, or what you

103

are doin'; and I don't know who I am, and
no one knows who they are. I almost believe
in God for this. Yes, I believe in God now;
and after all my search for happiness and
beauty, there is no time more beautiful than
this.' She put her arms around me; and
there we was, me who had stole the pie, and
Miss Siddons who had that face she couldn't
show, there on the Mississippi, cryin' and
wonderin', and yet happy, with a funny happiness that I don't understand.

"Well, the mornin' come and the Master
didn't come back. You feel different the next
day after you have made a promise like I
made Miss Siddons. I wasn't thinkin' of
goin' back on it; but the night before I kind
of wanted to go to jail for her; but in the
mornin' I didn't want to, I was only willin' to
like a feller is willin' to fight a boy that he
knows can lick him, and jest sails in for fear
of bein' a cowherd. So after breakfast Miss
Siddons said we must start; and she got me
to put the chicken coop in the wagon, with
the three chickens in it, and her dog, and
the chest with her things, and the rest of
the things that we could take; and so we

started, me not knowin' the road to Petersburg, and afraid that every time we asked it would excite suspicion on account of her with that veil, and on account of the chicken coop, the dog, the chest and all that funny stuff. Everybody looked at us, they laughed at us, and some yelled at us as we went along. And all I could do at first was jest to head north; for no one in this country knew about Petersburg or where it was. It was later that I began to ask about Petersburg and have people tell me who knowed livin' near or havin' been here.

"It took more'n a week to get here, and through a awful country part of the time, and bad roads, and the horse was slow. Of course we had to stop nights and make up a bed of quilts and things in the woods, and make fires and cook them chickens, which was a good thing; for then we threw away the coop which jostled around in the wagon. And so we went on; and finally one mornin' I began to know where I was a little from havin' drove around here some with Jim Riley which was the hired man of old Cap Proctor, who used to come for me to go with

him to the Cap's farms. And I was afraid
I'd see someone who knowed me, if we got into
town by daylight and so arrest me. And as
I hadn't told Miss Siddons about the pie, or
about being raised in Petersburg I had to
play tricks here by drivin' slower; for anyway the old horse was pretty tired. At about
sundown I said the horse had to rest, and so
we unhitched him, or I did, and let him eat
by the road and we went over into the woods
and rested up, and finally havin' the last
of the chickens. When it was about seven
o'clock we started again, and she knowed, too,
that we was pretty close to town, and I
thought she was pretty quiet and sad. And
jest as we turned around there by the mill,
comin' from Old Salem she wanted to know
if I wouldn't come to her house or her
mother's and stay for the night; and I said
that I wouldn't because I'd ruther sleep in
the woods. But what I meant to do was to
get right out of town, until I saw the lights
in your house, George. And though I told
her I'd see her the next mornin' I never expected to. For havin' got her safe home I
didn't think it made no difference whether

she ever saw me again or not. And that's why she didn't pay me nothin' when I left her after helpin' her in the house, because she expected to see me the next mornin'. Then I put up the horse, and come over to your house seein' it all lighted up. And if you hadn't been makin' wine I don't suppose there would have been lights.

"So that was the story as I told it to George, Eliza, Cora, Ernest Drew, and Joe Lester. And when I stopped and had told it all, Joe was sittin' leanin' over, his hands holdin' his knees tight, his eyes standin' out and his pointed ears up. And he says first before anyone else could speak: 'Kid, you'll never go to the Reformatory. I'll give these jays somethin' to think about before you do that. I'll go downtown and pick a deacon's pocket or rob the bank, and I'll do it so slick that the state's attorney will be all fall and winter gettin' the evidence; and I'll make an alibi that they will have some work to get around. I'll give these hunters somethin' to do; and if anyone goes behind the bars it will be me. I'm used to it; it don't bother me much; and I know how to saw out; and it's

107

my first chance to go to jail for somethin' besides the haul I make. You will go to the
Reformatory, Kid—over the left shoulder.'
Then George said, 'Over two left shoulders,'
jest as the doorbell rung and Miss Siddons'
servant came over and said that she had had
a letter from Dr. Walcott of Springfield and
wanted to see George about it. So we broke
up and I began to help Eliza and Cora."

## CHAPTER V

"SEVERAL days now went by, and I was still hidin' in George's house and wonderin' what was goin' to become of me; and I was busy helpin' Eliza with the house, while George was still sayin' that it would be over the left shoulder that I would go to the Reformatory. He must have told Miss Siddons that I was with him; or maybe Eliza did; for Miss Siddons come over one day, and after that come several times; I mean at night for she didn't want no one to see her face. But along about now Dr. Walcott came over from Springfield to see Miss Siddons, and she was now livin' in hope about her face, that she could show it even if it never was pretty enough again so that she could act on the stage. Finally George had got his papers ready and gone to Springfield to get the Governor to pardon George Heigold and Charley King. But before he went away there had come to George by the post office a report of the Reformatory, which he had give to Ernest to read; and so Ernest had read it, and showed it to Joe to see if Joe would say that the report was true about the things in prison; and him and Joe was talkin' this over lots in the evening, when we all set around, Cora and Eliza and the rest of us. Cora had been in the House of the Good Shepherd, as I have said; and in a general way all this interested her too.

"So one day Eliza put me up through the scuttle hole of the ceilin' to clean out the eaves which she said hadn't been cleaned, she believed since old Jeff Montgomery built the house. Joe and Ernest was in the room below visitin' and I could hear what they was sayin' without tryin' even to listen. Ernest was sayin' that Mr. Sprinkle would hardly speak to him, as well as George; and Joe said he knew that Mr. Sprinkle had threatened all kinds of things against him if George

110

didn't let up on havin' the boys pardoned; and that he was doin' all this so as to be known for a good prosecutor, so as to get a reputation and go to Congress or maybe be governor; for that's the way men rise in politics, Joe said. Then Ernest said that he had been on a newspaper, and that all the men on the newspaper knowed that the law was enforced mostly against boys and small criminals and that bankers and such didn't get it. So Ernest said that this here report of the Reformatory showed that ninety per cent of the boys in the Reformatory was there for what he said was property crimes, and that of course they stole or forged to get somethin' to live on; and as fur as that's concerned everybody was up to the property business in some way, bankers, lawyers and everything. He said that only a few was in for killin', cuttin', or fightin'; and that lots of 'em never drank, which showed that all the talk about likker and crime was stuff. And that as to religion and religious trainin' there was ministers' sons in there, and only 13 came from families that had no religion; and only 3 was sons of saloon-keepers out of 365 in

there; but most of 'em came from poor families, all but 61; and most of 'em had no
work when they got into trouble. So then
Ernest asked Joe to give him a pitcher of the
Reformatory. And Joe went on to say that
it was a world by itself; and that there might
be good guards, but it's a prison jest the
same; jest as you'd say this here is a hotel,
so you say this is a prison. He said you
have to get up at a certain time and work,
and then go to school; and that when they
feed the boys they march 'em into the dining-
room, and every boy carries his spoon—no
knife and no fork, jest a spoon. And they
pass two other boys behind a big tub, who
dip out stuff on your plate, hash or spaghetti,
which smells awful sometimes. Your bread
is on a plate on the table, and your pot of
tea or coffee, and so you set down and eat.
And then you go to your cell, if it's the end
of the day, which always ends when it's full
daylight, and there you stand in front of
your cell till the word is given. Then you
go in your cell; and all at once the lever
is pulled by one of the guards and all the
cells is shut at once; and there you are with

112

some other boy with two bunks, one over the other; and a wash bowl and a toilet and towels and things like that. And there you can read till they put the lights out for the night. Then you hear the guard walk by, for they watch you to see if anything is goin' on in the cells, and if there is they make it hot for you. So this was the life that George Heigold and Charley King was havin' for stealin' that pie! And was I goin' there, too?

"I couldn't see what made Mr. Sprinkle so mean, unless he wanted to be governor. So then Joe went on to say if you did anything they put you into the solitary. That made me listen more than ever. I quit workin' up there in the eaves and jest tried to hear every word Joe was tellin' about the solitary. He said it was a cell several stairs up, with no winder in it, and no light from anywheres, and no air except what come up through a hole in the floor. And they put you in there and lock the iron door, and slam a wooden door against the iron door, so that it is dark as the grave; and you can't hear nothin', only your own ears roarin'.

You have nothin' to set down on, and no place to lie down but the floor; and when you get all wored out you roll up in a blanket that they give you and go to sleep. Joe went on to say that he was in the solitary several times, but onct that he remembered for whippin' a cell-mate for somethin' awful this cell-mate did; and he said that the solitary will break the toughest kid you ever saw, and that it was the awfulest thing in the world. I was trimblin' now for thinkin' of what was ahead for me maybe; and wonderin' if I had been smart in bringin' Miss Siddons back, which of course I weren't if I had been thinkin' of myself. Joe then went on to say that you had church there, but you saw a lot of tough kids, and when you first go, bein' a beginner, they tell you lots of things, and pretty soon you get the idea of makin' this your life and graduatin' into the peniten-tiary, like you go up from the grammar school. Well, I was pretty near sick hearin' this, and I was wonderin' what luck George would have with gettin' the boys out, and if he got 'em out would Mr. Sprinkle quit on me. Maybe not. Maybe he'd say it warn't fair for me to get away and them to be punished, and so would go for me, bein' mad anyway that his work was upset by havin' the boys pardoned if they was. So I was worryin' and I came down out of the eaves feelin' pretty blue. Besides there I was in George's house, and couldn't go out except at night to walk around the yard with Joe or Ernest to get the air; and jest waitin' for George to come back, or get things fixed. Then as Miss Siddons knowed I was at George's house, maybe it wouldn't be long or hadn't been before the whole town would know I was there. So every time the bell rung I jumped thinkin' it was the sheriff. I lived sheriff and dreamed sheriff and couldn't eat sometimes for thinkin' of the sheriff.

"One night Miss Siddons came over to see Eliza. She never went out in the daytime no more than I did. Eliza had a letter that day from George from Springfield where he had been tryin' to see the governor, and was goin' to have a hard time, he thought, because Mr. Sprinkle had come there to argue with the governor about lettin' the boys out of the Reformatory. This night Joe and

Ernest was not at home havin' gone to help
find Dr. Powell who had disappeared. They
was sayin' that he had jumped into one of
the old coal mines, and this night they was
goin' to let somebody down to the bottom of
the mine to see if they could find the body.
That's how Joe and Ernest happened to be
away, when Miss Siddons come to see Eliza.

"You see Eliza had always been for church,
and Miss Siddons hadn't, and they was never
friends; but now Eliza seemed to be sorry
for Miss Siddons, and besides she knowed that
George wanted her to be, so she was good to
her, and talked to her as nice as could be.
Cora Dunleavy had gone to bed early, and
so that left me and Eliza and Miss Siddons
alone together. She had found out by now
that my name was Kit and not Conrad, so
she called me that, and laughed from behind
her veil, and seemed in better spirits than
what she had been down on the Mississippi.
First she said that she had allus dreaded to
have her face cut or anythin', but she had
knowed that it had to be done all the time,
and that Dr. Walcott said so and that she
was goin' to do it; and that he said while

116

she wouldn't be very beautiful after it, she wouldn't be so very awful either. She was sayin' that the reason she had never done anythin' was on account of bein' down-hearted, and really sick in bed, besides havin' the Master on her hands and then gettin' into that life on the river, which was the craziest thing of her whole crazy life. She talked jest that way of her life; it had always been crazy, and she thought everyone's is if you look right into it. She said when she was travelin' in boats and trains, in America, China and Europe that she often thought she'd be drownded, or killed in a wreck; but she never dreamed she'd be back to Petersburg like this, where she had tried to keep away from, on account of the way the people had treated her. And then she said plainer: 'The funniest thing of all, Eliza, is that I should be talkin' here to you, for we was never much friends and I always felt that you looked on me like all the church people did.' And Eliza said it was true. 'You never liked me, Eliza,' said Miss Siddons; and Eliza said calm like, 'I never approved of you, Julia.' 'Well,' said Miss Siddons, 'who

117

knows who will take care of 'em at the last?
It's more likely to be people who was never
your friends before than the folks you have
allus chummed with. Maybe that's because
the people that was your chums die quicker
or go away sommers.' And Eliza said,
'Yes.'

"Then Miss Siddons said that it warn't
just havin' fun and lookin' for fun that had
made trouble for her, but that it was tryin'
to rise in the world. And that she was sure
that Petersburg had been down on her as
much for that as anythin', or more; and had
even used these other things against her, like
havin' parties at her pap's house when she
used to come back in the summers, and ridin'
about with her beaux from New York and all
that, to hide what they envied because she
had been to England and had almost riz to
the top as a actress. She had already spoke
of the Master, and now Eliza wanted to know
about him; for she could see that Miss Siddons was not clear crazy and never had been;
and yet how would she marry the Master,
seein' that she could get along somehow, by
even sellin' that emerald ring if no other

118

way? Besides the Master earned nothin'
anyway. It was all crazy. So Miss Siddons
began to tell the story, which I had never
heard from this side before; and I was lyin'
now on the couch pretendin' to be asleep.
Miss Siddons said that she first knowed the
Master a long while ago when he was young
and fine to look at and was makin' some
money as a actor; and that it was jest after
the duke, that I have already told about bein'
divorced from her, had gone to Canada. She
said that the Master was never much of a
actor, but had tried to play Shakespeare and
couldn't; and that he was so bad in the
*Count of Monte Cristo* that you'd almost
laugh yourself to death to see him. And still
he tried with all his might and never seemed
to give up. She said they had went with
each other lots in San Francisco, and that he
wanted to marry her then, which she wouldn't.
She said that this bad face began to come
on her after she had a spell of sickness in
New Orleans, havin' scratched her face one
day with a pin in a curtain which had fell off
the rod when she was tryin' to pull the curtain down, and that the pin had pisened her

face, so that when she got up out of bed from the pisen she had her face all splotched and so had to begin to wear a veil. She said that she met the Master in San Francisco fifteen years ago; and that it was a year ago that she was sick from the scratched face. And that one day when she had got up from bed and was out walkin' there in New Orleans the Master come along, and follered her. And that because she was as bad off as him, or worse, and because he said all kinds of things to her about takin' care of her that it won her; besides his sayin' that they would be on the Mississippi in a house-boat, and live outdoors healthy and so both get well. She said it was awful in the boardin' house in New Orleans; and besides as soon as she could walk the landlady began to say that she wanted her to move and find another place to live; and after all she was wonderin' if she wouldn't jest be drove from place to place on account of her face. So she said it was all so crazy that nothin' mattered; and havin' knowed the Master all these years she thought she'd marry him and take to the woods this-a-way. Then Eliza began to say

120

that she must have knowed that her mother
was here and that she had a good home here
to rest up in, and asked her why she didn't
come back to Petersburg, instead of marryin'
the Master and goin' in that awful house-
boat. Then Miss Siddons said that she
couldn't bear to come back here where the
people said that she had broke her father's
heart, and shamed her mother, and come back
with a face which said that she had done jest
that. She said she couldn't bear to come back
where she had never had any praise for tryin'
to rise in the world, but where everybody believed that she was jest a butterfly tryin'
to have nothin' but pleasure; and where no
one believed that she had ever succeeded;
and she said that she thought most little
towns in America was a curse. Then she
said that this was jest the place for the
Master to return to, if this had been his
home town, since he had turned to preachin',
and forcin' people to do what he believed
was right, havin' failed as a actor; but as for
herself she had not changed her ideas about
life at all, and never would as long as she
lived; that if she had come home to die she

121

would die game, never confessin' to Petersburg that she had taken the wrong path in life, and they the right, which they had tried so hard to get her to foller. 'No sir,' she says, 'I'll die game; and if I don't die, and since I am caught back here, I'll show these people what it is to make the best of things when you are down and out, not after livin' here all your life; but after havin' seed everythin' in the world. Maybe I can do somethin' for Conrad, or show some girl here that she must have her own ideas if they are for beautiful things and life and stick to 'em.'

"That seemed to remind Eliza that there was somethin' between their families anyway, for she said that her father thought the world of Miss Siddons' father, which was one of the finest men in the world; and she told Miss Siddons that she remembered her when she was a little girl, meanin' when Eliza was; for Miss Siddons was maybe ten year older than Eliza, and so was jest about ten when Miss Siddons first came back from bein' in the theater; and Eliza said that she used to be awful fussed up hearin' about

Miss Siddons and seein' her when she come back, until she began to hear talk, and especially hear the minister and the Sunday School superintendent talk, onct, when Miss Siddons was here and had a party on her lawn on Sunday, with some music and lots of talk and laughin'. Then Miss Siddons went on to talk about her failure and all that.

" 'Well, Eliza, what's the use of my foolin' myself,' says she. 'I could have riz to the top if I had the mind. I had chance enough. I don't whine about what they done to me, and say I could have riz except for that; for if I had the mind to get up, I would have had the mind to keep people from keepin' me from gettin' up. Anyway I say that. Of course marriages is always dangerous for anybody, and I had four dangers: the cornet player, one that didn't count at all and I never think about, then a rich man out west, and he left me because I wouldn't quit actin'; and finally the Master. What's all this talk about me bein' so bad, Eliza? I married all of 'em, didn't I? And if marriage is such a grand thing, I have honored it more than anyone most in Petersburg by goin' into it so many

123

times. Well, I have a better reason about marryin', and that is it mixes happiness with work, and it can't be done; and whenever I did that I sinned and had trouble. This thing of tryin' to get love and believin' in it as I did will get anybody into trouble. Then the wrinkles come on me, and instead of tryin' to make my work better in spite of wrinkles, which can be painted out, I tried to make my face prettier. That's where I sinned, Eliza, until I come right down where the Master could pick me up on the streets of New Orleans and make it interestin' to me to go on a house-boat. You see then I didn't know he was crazy about preachin'. His hair was not much longer than when he played Shakespeare. But we no sooner got started up the river than he had to stop and get out to preach and get ready for Judgment Day; to stop all the way up to near St. Louis. And then I saw he was clean crazy, and that I was in for somethin' worse than I had ever been.'

"So then Eliza let Julia know that she knew about the ring which the Master had throwed away; and so Miss Siddons told

Eliza all about it from the beginnin', jest
as I told it. Only she said somethin' new,
which was that the ring had been give her
by the rich man she was married to, and that
the Master was jealous and all his talk about
the sin of her havin' the ring was jest stuff,
and bein' a hypocrite, which he was.

"I was lyin' there listenin' but at last almost goin' to sleep, because lots of this was
old to me. And I was jest in a doze, when
I heard George's voice. He had come in quiet
and jest said hello in a tired voice to everybody. Eliza jumped up to hear the news;
and the first thing that George said was to
show us the St. Louis paper where it had in
big type these words: 'Burglars Loosed on
Petersburg Community.' George Heigold
and Charley King had been pardoned by the
governor, and this was what welcomed them
to the town that they was goin' to try to live
a good life in. 'Ain't that devilish?' said
George, mad and tired. 'Mr. Sprinkle wrote
that for the paper. He was whipped out before the governor, and this is his revenge.'
So then Eliza put her arms around George
and told him not to worry; and Miss Siddons

said he was the best man in the world; and now she was goin' to help him raise me and George and Charley, havin' nothin' better to do. We was all crazy to hear how George had got the boys out; but Miss Siddons had to go home, and George had to take her. Eliza told me to go to bed, and I did, worryin' about Mr. Sprinkle. For if he would have a thing like that printed about two boys who was let out to be good and go on in the world what wouldn't he do to me? I stood at the winder lookin' out into the night. Then I looked at the sheets on the bed. It would have been easy to make a rope of the sheets and slip down to the ground and jest run off. I was about to do it, when I got to thinkin' of Miss Siddons who had come back here to live her life and do the best she could; and about George who was makin' such a fight for me. So I said no to myself and went to bed, and dreamed all night of the sheriff."

under the wheels by the brakeman; and that
it was all over Petersburg that these boys
had been arrested for the pie a good deal
more for gettin' them out of the way, the railroad doin' it, than it was about the pie. This
made Mr. Sprinkle awful mad; and he said
that it was a reflection upon the judge and
him to say such things, and a reflection upon
the law, which was justice, and that if it
was true that the railroad wanted to get these
boys out of the way, it was true that the
railroad had the grounds to get 'em out of the
way on; and that the boys had done burglary
and been found guilty of burglary, and had
no right to say that they was really sent
to prison for knowin' how another boy got
kilt. And Mr. Sprinkle went on and said
that it was silly to talk about a pie, and
sendin' boys to prison for a pie; that all that
was jest the talk of a man who harbored
criminals and who didn't respect the law
hisself; that what these boys had done was to
break into a house, and that if they had only
took a pin after breakin' in it would be as
much burglary as if they had stole diamonds,
and that any lawyer would say so; and that
131

the governor, who had been a lawyer, knew
that this was the law.   Then George said that
Mr. Sprinkle had him there, for he didn't
know whether that was the law or not, but
only that if it was it was foolish; and that
he told the governor that, and that he also
said that he knowed somethin' about killin'
people, and that the brakeman who knocked
Mitch under the wheels was guilty of killin'
him, and that it would be as well to arrest
the brakeman for that in this great work of
enforcin' the law as to arrest boys for a pie,
burglary or no burglary.

"So then George said he took up about the
cigarettes, for the State's attorney had
talked bitter about all of us smokin', sayin'
that there should be a law to do away with
terbacker in every form, and that boys who
smoked would drink or rob.   George said he
was ready for this with affidavits, showin'
that we bought the cigarettes, as I have already told; and he said he told the governor
that the cigarettes and the learnin' Mitch
Miller to flip cars had nothin' to do with the
pie, and was jest throwed in to make everythin' look worse, and to make us look bad.

Then the governor said that we had never been charged in court with the cigarettes or anythin', but the farmer's house and the pie, and he wouldn't consider such things. Mr. Sprinkle was gettin' madder and madder, and he said awful bitter things after sayin' again that the judge who tried 'em hadn't signed no papers to let 'em out; and then he yelled that even the fathers and mothers of the boys hadn't asked to get 'em out, and that George was jest a busybody, with no interest in the case at all, except to upset the law and make it disrespected. 'How are you going to make people respect the law?' he asked, in a awful loud voice, George said. 'By makin' the law respectable,' said George, and so they had it. Then George returned to the parents of George and Charley not askin' for them to get out, and said that it was true that their pas didn't care, one bein' a drunkard and no good, and the other dead, and no mother for George but only for Charley, who had been worked upon by someone to say that it would be good for her boy to be locked up where he couldn't get into trouble and where he would learn religion

133

and geogafy and things. Mr. Sprinkle
wound up by sayin' that George had now a
criminal turned over to him, which was Joe
Lester, one of the worst pickpockets in the
country; and that at this rate if George and
Charley was pardoned Petersburg would be
the greatest layin' up place for criminals in
America; and that the good people of Petersburg objected; that the voters of the town
objected to havin' their town made such a
place; and he went over the ground that he
had went over already, that me and the other
boys had entered the farmer's house to take
whatever we could find, and that it was no
fault of ourn that we hadn't found nothin'
but a pie. That law was law, and he was
swore to enforce it; and he would if the
whole state did not come for him with its
power and undo his work as fast as he had
done it. So then the governor seemed to
get tired; and Mr. Sprinkle saw it and said
that's all he had to say. 'That's all he had
to say,' said Eliza, kind of sneery; 'as if it
warn't enough.' For by this time Eliza was
likin' me and I believe she took no stock in
the idea that I would really steal. 'Yep,' says

134

George, 'Mr. Sprinkle set down now, and the governor just pressed a button, and a man come in with a book who wrote down what the governor said, which was that George Heigold and Charley King was pardoned. Then Mr. Sprinkle got up again and said that the people of Petersburg would be better pleased if they was jest let loose, to be sent back if they did any other crime, and that Mr. Montgomery who had gone into the business of takin' care of such boys and people would be a good man to turn 'em over to. So the governor said no, and that he believed a wrong had been done the boys by sendin' 'em to prison at all, where they had been several weeks; and that he wanted the boys to feel that they was pardoned of all wrong, and to start over again; and that he believed from the pitchers of the boys that they was good boys havin' good heads and good faces, not bad or criminals; and he wanted 'em to have a fresh start. So George said the governor shook his head firm, and Mr. Sprinkle set down kind of limp; and so the man come back with the pardon, and the

135

governor gave it to George who went to
Pontiac to get the boys out.

"So George said when he got to Pontiac
the warden was awful nice to him, and
showed him everythin' about the prison: the
cell houses, the dining-room, the work rooms,
the school room, the chapel, the yard where
the boys was stood in line like soldiers; and he
saw the walls where the guards was walkin'
ready to kill any boy who tried to get out.
It was worktime and there was only a few
boys in the cells. They was the crazy boys,
awful lookin' boys to see, with little heads,
and sick slow eyes, and yaller faces; and
there was one, George said, big and fat,
lookin' like a kangaroo, with a small head
about the size of a tea cup toppin' a long
thick neck. Then George saw the row of
cells, and the lever that closed 'em in all at
onct, just as Joe Lester said. At the noon-
hour George said the whistles blew mourn-
ful, and all the boys was brought in the big
yard with the walls around it, where a drum
was beat by one of the boys; and all the boys
then stood in line and waited for the word to
go to the dining-room. And George said

136

some of 'em was pretty bad lookin' boys, some bad niggers and all that, and one Chinaman; and ranged from twelve years old to sixteen maybe, or more. Then the word was give and they marched to the dinin'-room, takin' their food as they passed the tubs of stuff where the boys with ladles stood, just as Joe had told about, and true in every word accordin' to Joe. Then George said while standin' by the door watchin' this business he saw George Heigold and Charley King for the first. They got their food and went to their seats at the long wooden table, and set down by boys which looked pretty bad. And pretty soon a prayer was said by a preacher, and then the noise of eatin' filled the room. George said the smell of the food and the looks of the boys made him almost sick, so he turned away, and went with the warden back to his office. It was now that the warden sent for the papers about George and Charley and showed the letters which had been wrote by Mr. Sprinkle when George and Charley was sent to prison, where Mr. Sprinkle had said the meanest things about 'em to the warden, which the warden said he

137

believed until he had seen for hisself and knew that they was good boys. For the warden said that there was no better boys than them in the prison and never had been; and anybody could see that they was nothin' wrong with their heads; and that they had good teeth and good mouth roofs and ears and eyes and he was glad they was to be let out. So then George said the warden sent for George and Charley; and pretty soon a guard came bringin' 'em to the office, where the warden shut the door. And then they saw George and, of course, knew him, and began to look funny, but didn't speak because they was not allowed to. Then the warden spoke up and says to the boys: 'Do you know this man here?' And they nodded kind of humble and scared, but didn't speak, till the warden said, 'You can talk if you want to.' So they said 'yes, sir'; and the warden asked 'em how they would like to go back to Petersburg with Mr. Montgomery; and then George Heigold begun to cry; and Charley King looked down and didn't say nothin', jest pushed the carpet with his feet till he begun to cry, too, not

**138**

out loud, but with tears runnin' down his face. So then the warden said that they was suits for 'em and a little money and to go with the guard and get dressed and come back, and go with George back to Petersburg because they was pardoned. Then George said he brought 'em back to Petersburg on the train, and that was all of the story, except that George said that I had a lot to do with George and Charley gettin' out. 'How?' says I. 'Why,' says George, 'if you hadn't come back when you did I wouldn't have took up this business of gettin' 'em out for some time. It made me mad about them seein' you.' So I said, put it on to Miss Siddons; for she got me to bring her back to Petersburg; and except for her I wouldn't ever come back here.

"So now it was about nine o'clock and we was jest gettin' ready to go to bed. I was sick of everythin' and sure that somethin' would happen to me with Mr. Sprinkle so mad about the other boys bein' pardoned. I jest could feel it. And jest then the bell rang and Eliza went to the door. Pretty soon she came back into the room, her face

as white as a sheet, and she said, 'You'll
have to attend to this, George. Go to the
door.' 'What's the matter?' said George,
and he hurried to the door. Then he come
back with the sheriff follerin' him. They
had come for me. He had a warrant for
me breakin' in the farmer's house, and he
read it to me; and George says, 'That's all
right, Sheriff.' And so the sheriff took me,
and George went with me to sign my bond,
leavin' Eliza cryin', and Cora; and Joe and
Ernest swearin' like everythin'. When I got
to the sidewalk there was a carriage and
another officer and in the carriage was
George Heigold and Charley King. They
had been took from the farm where they was
workin' and arrested for breakin' the furniture in the jail when they was waitin' for
their trial about the pie, before they went
to the Reformatory. So Mr. Sprinkle was
enforcin' the law; and down all of us went
to the judge's office where George signed
bonds for all of us; and then we come back
and went to bed. But George was sayin'
all the way back to the house that he was
goin' to send for Hardy Kirby and show

Mr. Sprinkle a thing or two. I believed in George; but I felt so sick and funny I can't hardly describe it. I went to bed and slept; for jest to be arrested was to have that off your mind. Do you think the boys told the sheriff or someone I was at George's house? I don't know . . . I don't know to this day."

## CHAPTER VII

"You may think I was sorry for bein' arrested; but I warn't. I was glad. The burden was took off me at last of hidin', and I felt like Joe Lester said you feel when you go to the penitentiary, where everything is done for you and there is nothin' more to worry about. Joe Lester said that day that lots of fellers that could get away, get tired of hidin' and waitin' and so give theirselves up jest to get things ended. And that's the way I felt.

"Another thing, I didn't feel right with George and Charley goin' to the Reformatory and me livin' easy with nothin' to happen to me; and now if they had been took for breakin' the chairs, and furniture, and

142

I had been left alone even for the pie I
would have felt like a cowherd.  So takin'
everythin' together I was glad the sheriff
got me.  I could go out now and do anythin' I wanted to; I could go over to see
Miss Siddons which I did almost the first
thing, and she knew about me bein' arrested,
for that day the Petersburg paper had a
piece about all of us, sayin' like the St.
Louis paper did that burglars had been let
out on Petersburg, referrin' to George and
Charley; and sayin' about me, 'Kit O'Brien
comes back and is arrested for burglary.'
Well, that kind of cut, seein' the big type
and everythin'.  But Miss Siddons said to
laugh at it; that she had been arrested onct
in New York, not for burglary, but for
laughin' too loud and singin' too loud comin'
down Fifth Avenue one night; and that most
everybody got arrested onct in their lives,
same as havin' measles or somethin'.  When
I showed the piece in the paper to Joe he
jest looked at it same as a collie would look
at it, and said, 'Well, they got it right, ain't
they?' meanin' that they did arrest me, not,
of course, that I was a burglar.  I don't

believe Joe would care for any printin' about him no matter what it was; that's why he looked like a collie at what they printed about me.

"George told me to go wherever I wanted to and to do anything, but to be careful not to get into no fights or anythin', because it would make it harder for me. So when I went over to see my pap one day I jest had to let some kids whistle at me and say 'yah' 'yah' about my bein' arrested, and wait till I was out of the woods before wadin' into 'em for that insult. My pap warn't much glad to see me. He was sleepin' when I got to the house, all wrapped up in quilts, for he had took a job of night watch at the woolen mill, and so slept in the day. He jest looked at me and said somethin' about my bein' in some trouble; and he asked me where I was livin', and then lit his pipe and looked stiddy before him and didn't say nothin'. Parents is like freckles or cross eyes or anythin': you jest have 'em; but because you do it's no sign that you ought to. So I left him and went down the hill to Fillmore's Woods for a bit which I hadn't seed

144

since the early spring before, and walked up and down lookin' at the trees and wonderin' why trees was or men or anythin', includin' jails and sheriffs and all that.

"George and Charley had gone back to the farm to work, because the trial warn't for some time and we didn't know when it would be. George had sent for Hardy Kirby to defend us, and he lived in another county and wouldn't come till later; but also the state's attorney was pretty busy with something else, which was that Mr. Tallman which owned the big store and several rich men in Petersburg had failed and closed their stores and banks on account of notes they had to pay to a Peoria bank, which they had give to a man named Walter Rice who had come to Petersburg and sold stock in a coperation for the notes, and then gone to Peoria and sold the notes to the bank; and as the stock was no good they had busted and had to close up. This is what George said. But Miss Siddons told me, too, when I was over to her house helpin' her, which I did considerable when Eliza didn't want me; and it was then that Miss Siddons showed

145

me more things out of her chest which she
hadn't finished when we was down on the
Mississippi. Miss Siddons had knowed this
Walter Rice, as he was about her age; and
she said that the people in Petersburg had
treated him jest like they treated her, especially the deacons and such, which Mr.
Tallman was; and that he had took revenge
on 'em by sellin' 'em stock in this coperation,
which wasn't cattle or anything alive, but
pieces of paper. Miss Siddons said that
this here Walter Rice was almost drove out
of Petersburg by these deacons and things,
because he was a dancer and smoked and
used to play the banjo; and that finally
about the time that she went on the stage
he had gone away, too, and she hadn't heard
of him all these years, except maybe that
he was in Colorado or sommers. George
knowed everythin' and he heard everythin'
and when he come home one night he told all
of us that the truth was that Mr. Tallman
and the bank and all these men supposed to be
rich had been runnin' on thin ice for a long
while; and all that this Walter Rice had
done was just to breathe on the ice which

146

was so rotten that it melted with his breath, and let 'em all down in the water. This had happened about the time we stole the pie and run away, I mean Walter sellin' this stock in the coperation; but it had jest come out now when these men bust.

"This here Walter Rice had come to Petersburg and the first thing put $15,000 in the bank, which was somethin' that set the town crazy, it was so much money, and set everybody wonderin'. But he didn't say nothin', but was visitin' with relatives on the farm, and didn't come to town, except to church on Sunday when he put $10 in the contribution, and onct at prayer meetin' which was Wednesday night, he had prayed and made a talk. Then one day he went into Mr. Tallman's store and he was awful curious about Walter and this $15,000 and wanted to know what Walter was doin' for a livin', and how he had become so rich since he left Petersburg. You see everybody was awful polite to him now, and nobody remembered that he used to play the banjo and dance, and all that, which he said he hadn't done, talkin' one day to lots of men in Mr. Tallman's store,

since he jined the church. So they kept
teasin' him, and finally he told 'em that he
was president of the American Reduction
Company, which made copper from clay, by
extractin' the copper from the clay by a
patent thing; and that he had stopped off in
the dear old town of his boyhood to see all
the folks before goin' to New York to live.
It warn't long before Mr. Tallman and the
others wanted to buy some of this stock, but
Walter wouldn't sell, sayin' that there was
none for sale and that it had all been took,
and that what he had he wanted for hisself,
and couldn't sell. Well he went along teasin'
this way, till finally he had sold Mr. Tallman
$50,000 worth and some others around that
much or more, and took their notes for it,
which he had sold to the Peoria bank, and got
the money before goin' to New York to live.
So when the Peoria bank, which thought the
notes good when buyin' 'em, because everybody believed Mr. Tallman was awful rich,
wanted to get the money on the notes from
Mr. Tallman and the rest, they couldn't pay,
and had busted and closed up. So Mr.
Sprinkle, the state's attorney, was pretty

busy with this business and tryin' to keep Mr.
Tallman and the others out of jail, because
they was after 'em, people was, who had lost
their money, because they bust; and Mr.
Sprinkle was sayin' that they had been
wronged, and had done nothin' wrong theirselves; and the bank had done nothin' wrong
for acceptin' money from people to keep,
when the bank was in trouble and about to
bust and really owed more'n it could pay;
because the law which said that banks mustn't
take money from people to keep for them
when it is in debt itself and owes more'n it
can pay was unconstitutional, or somethin';
and that he was swore to support the constitution and was goin' to do it. And as for
goin' after this here Walter Rice there was
no law to do it by, because he had sold real
stock in a real coperation; and if the thing,
whatever it was, wouldn't fetch the copper
out of clay, that's somethin' that Mr. Tallman and others should have looked into to
know for theirselves, same as buyin' a horse
or anything else. All this George told us,
and said that they was afraid to go after
Walter; that they was all so shamed of bein'

149

skinned by him that they was glad to let it rest and die out. And so, as George said, none of this here was plain and clear like a pie case. Well, all this was keepin' the state's attorney busy; and so George and Charley was not tried for breakin' the furniture in the jail, and I warn't tried for the pie; and so the weeks went by.

"Miss Siddons laughed herself most to death when she heard the whole story about Walter Rice, and she said that it seemed like gods havin' fun with folks that after all these years Walter should more'n get even on these old thieves and such; for that's what she called 'em. She considered that they had been mean to her too, and had a lot to do with her life by makin' her have bad feelin's and moods when she was here, or even when she was away; for she said that she never got so far away from Petersburg that it didn't have a kind of hold on her; she was either despisin' the town, or else she was sub- mittin' to it, and tryin' not to. Miss Siddons was gettin' in better spirits every day now; for Dr. Walcott was comin' to see her, and one day she showed me a little of her face

150

and said, 'Look Conrad,' and I did; and it
looked to me like it was gettin' better, and I
said so. 'Gettin' better,' says she laughin'.
'Ah, there, Judith Siddons,' says she, 'you
may make it yet.' And so about now she
was walkin' out on her lawn sometimes, and
had give up only goin' out at night, which she
did at first, as I have told. So one day she
asked me this: 'What do you think has become of the Master, Conrad?' says she.
'Gone to heaven, maybe,' says I. 'I hope so,'
says she; 'for maybe he'll want to stay there;
and if he don't they won't let him out anyway.'

"So between goin' to the farm with George,
helpin' Eliza and Miss Siddons, and all that
the days passed; and I was goin' downtown
considerable and people was beginnin' to be
good to me, not sayin' that anyone had ever
been very bad. But I begun to see people
like McLean Watkins and that Kay Watkins
that had the house by the store on the Sangamon River, and some of the Atterberrys and
such, which was friendly people and knowed
me and talked to me friendly; besides Jack
McHenry which was a awful fighter with fists

or bricks or anything, and said that I ought
to get a brick and lay Mr. Sprinkle out;
and that if he had done to him what Mr.
Sprinkle had done to me and to George and
Charley he would have beat his head off; that
onct he had stobbed a man here, and Mr.
Sprinkle only had him fined for it, and here
we had been in all this trouble for a pie; and
that the way to use state's attorneys was to
make 'em afraid of you, or else to buy 'em,
or else to belong to the same church with 'em.
And he told me to pluck up and all would
be all right with me.

"And one day I was downtown, I was right
there where Cave Sanford had his store,
which was not a store any more for groceries,
but they played pool in there now, because
Cave had been dead long before I was born;
and I saw Mr. Sprinkle the state's attorney
over in front of the drug store on the North
side of the square talkin' to a man, a funny
lookin' man; and it seemed that there was
somethin' about this man that I knowed; so
I looked closer; and jest then Mr. Sprinkle
pointed toward me, and this here funny

lookin' man started to come where I was. So I went in the poolroom and out the back door into the alley, and then to the street and up the hill to George's house runnin' as fast as I could. Don't think I was afeard. It warn't that; but I wanted to get to George's and tell him; so I bust into the kitchen where George and Eliza was, and Cora, Joe and Ernest bein' out sommers; and I said, catchin' my breath, 'He's here . . . he's. . . .' 'Who?' said George. 'The Master,' says I. 'I jest saw him, and I think he's comin' here.' So then Eliza sank into a chair and said, 'George! I simply won't have that creature in my house. . . . I won't!' 'Can't he sleep in the barn?' said George, kind of smilin'. 'No,' says Eliza; 'he can't sleep in the barn or anywhere near the barn or this house.' 'Well, listen,' says George, 'we may have to do somethin' with him on account of Julia; we can't let him go to her. We got to do somethin'.' So Eliza almost cried, she sighed and jest wrung her hands, maybe because she thought she had enough on her hands with me and Cora and

153

Joe. So George kept lookin' out of the winder; and pretty soon we saw someone; and it was the Master comin' along, walkin' fast, his long hair wavin' and as he got closer we could see how dusty he was. So George started for the front door, with Eliza follerin' him and beggin' him not to take the Master in, till he promised he wouldn't. I was follerin' too. And jest then Ernest come in, and George called to him to come along. When the Master lifted the latch of the gate to come in the yard, George walked out onto the porch with Ernest, and me close by, because George had said he wanted me with 'em; and so we went out on the walk meetin' the Master as he came along; and finally takin' his hand and sayin' 'howdy.' So the Master called me a little scamp for runnin' away from him; and told me to run in the house and get him some water, and kind of ordered me around, as if we was still on the boat in the Mississippi; and so I run and got the water; and when I got back I heard George say to him to come in the house, as it was a little cool outside; and so we was about to go, with Eliza dis-

154

Ernest kind of watchin' him, and I knowed
that if he tried to do anything to me, that
they would stop him. Then he got to talkin'
about that emerald ring and wanted to know
if I had dived for it, and I said no, and of
course lied, because I had as I have already
told; and I said it warn't any use to dive
for it on account of the muddy bottom of the
Mississippi, which he said he knowed, havin'
dived for it hisself when he come back to the
house-boat, and couldn't find it. 'It's a good
riddance,' he said, 'and has gone down with
the eels and the snakes, and the turtles.'

"Finally the Master said that he wanted to
go over and see the house that his wife had
inherited; and I looked to see what George
would say to this. And George said jest as
calm as before that Miss Siddons had the
key, and that when she come back termorrow
that they would all go over and see it. Somethin' else seemed to come into the Master's
mind now; for he got up and walked about
the room, awful nervous, with George and
Ernest both watchin' him, as I was too, for
fear he might jump on me suddenly and try
to do somethin' to me. Then after a bit he

159

come and set down again and twisted his
fingers, and talked to hisself, and began to
tell us how the Lord guided him to this town;
that he knowed Miss Siddons had come here
to her fine house; he knowed she had money,
which she was hidin'; and that when he got
to Petersburg he met the state's attorney
right away, who told him that George Montgomery had plenty of beds and food, and
would take him in, as he took in everybody;
and that George could tell him where Miss
Siddons was if she was in town at all. And
that the state's attorney had pointed me out
to him and told him to foller me and so come
to George's house; and that he had done it,
and it was the Lord who had guided him
to Petersburg, all the way from St. Louis and
straight to George's house, where his wife
was. So I saw that he believed this; but
suppose that Miss Siddons had come, or had
come out on her lawn, and he had been at
the winder and seed her? I was settin' on
the edge of my chair, as scared as if a cannon
was about to bust there, not knowin' what
would happen next. All the while George
was rockin' and talkin' to the Master, and

160

keepin' him interested; and I could see George was thinkin' what was best to do with this awful crazy man. Eliza must have been worried out of her head upstairs, or wherever she was, while all this was goin' on. So then George asked him how he got to Petersburg, and the Master said he walked from St. Louis, where he had went to be crucified; but when he got in the city, the Lord told him that his time had not yet come, and to go back to the house-boat; and that he did go back and found it empty and everything gone; and then he said he suspicioned with his mortal mind that Miss Siddons had gone back to Petersburg to her mother's house; and while he was thinkin' this the Lord came to him in a vision and showed him the house, and that it was jest like the house itself; and he claimed now that he knowed that Miss Siddons' mother was dead, that the Lord had told him so; and that he must not yet be crucified, but must go to Miss Siddons and help her and take care of her, and sacrifice for her, and that was the way of truth and of life, and that he had lived in sin as a actor seekin' happiness, until the Lord showed

161

him the truth and told him to live for and
to seek the truth, and to die for it and to
preach it before he was crucified, and to make
the world see it, whether it wanted to or
not. And he said that he was married to
Miss Siddons the same as the angels in heaven
marry, which was pure marriage and without
sin, and that he had always been married to
her that way, and that their love was the same
as Christ's love for the church. Then he
asked George if he was married and George
said yes; but that it was a sinful marriage,
and he meant to change it and make it a
speeritual marriage, which was what his wife
wanted. Ernest laughed now, laughed out
loud, and the Master got mad and asked
what the matter was and Ernest said that
George didn't have the religious nature to
make it a speeritual marriage; and so the
Master wanted to pray with George, and
George let him; and then the Master closed
his eyes and prayed to hisself, while the rest
of us set as still as mice watchin' to see what
he would do next.

"Then George said that he thought it was
the work of God that the Master had come

agin me and was jest foolin' before. Finally
he wanted more coffee and Mrs. Potter give
it to him, and more cake and she give him
that; and he went on eatin' while the men was
talkin' about farm things, and such as that.
After a bit I began to notice that the Master's head was droopin'; and one of the
Potter boys edged over seein' that the cup
and saucer was tiltin' out of his hand, and
jest caught it in time to keep it from fallin'
to the floor. Then George winked at old man
Potter, and laughed a little, and I looked at
the Master, and his head was over on one
side, and he was about asleep. If I had
ever seed him asleep before I never had no-
ticed him as I did now; but now his forehead
seemed so white and high, and his nose was
so thin and kind of like a woman's; and I
could see his mouth between his beard, which
looked like a woman's too. So there we set
and rocked, and said nothin'. It must have
been more'n fifteen minutes; and the Master
was clear gone. His head was down on his
breast and he was sound asleep. So then
George said, 'We're all ready.' And one of
the Potter boys went out and come back with

two big strops. He knelt down and buckled one of 'em around his legs, and the Master didn't know about it or do a thing. Then he buckled the other around his waist, tyin' his arms this-a-way tight to his side. At this Joe kind of give a jump, because as he told me afterwards that's the way they do when men is hung. But George was smilin', not a mean smile, but a smile which meant that he had done what he wanted to. So after the Master was all buckled and didn't wake up, George said, 'Come on.'

"So the two Potter boys got hold of the Master and lifted him up and began to carry him. He kind of come to now and began to mutter, but not much. And so they carried him out to the carriage, with him mutterin' some, but in a weak voice that you couldn't understand. But he was not fightin' because he couldn't, and seemed too sleepy. It was awful excitin' now for me, and so I asked George what they was goin' to do with him; but George jest said, 'You're goin' to get to see, get in the front seat and set on the lap of Jim Potter.' I did. Joe was drivin'. And in the back seat there was George and

168

Ernest, with the Master between 'em, sound asleep, and harmless as a tired chicken.

"Joe was tappin' the horses and we was just goin' along through a country I never had seed before, and right away from Petersburg. Till finally, after about a hour, I saw signs of a town, advertisin' where to buy things and names that didn't belong to Petersburg; and George said we're pretty near there. And finally we drove into a town where there was a court-house. And I says to George, 'What is this?' And he says, 'This is Virginia, the County Seat of Cass County.' Well, I begun to wonder now more'n ever. And suddenly we drove to a stone house, and I looked up and saw iron bars and knowed it was a jail. Then George got out, and the Potter boy and Ernest, leavin' me and Joe in the carriage. And they lifted the Master out who was still asleep, and the Potter boy took him on his shoulder like a sack of wheat, with the Master grumblin' a little, and carried him to the door of the jail. Just then the sheriff come out, and George shook his hand, and seemed to know him; and they talked, and the sheriff looked

169

at the Master and waved his hand. So the door was opened and I saw the Master carried into the jail.

" 'What's he arrested for?' says I to Joe. 'Cracked,' says Joe. 'Well, ain't that funny that he was so sound asleep that he didn't know?' 'George fixed him all right,' says Joe. Just then George and Ernest and the Potter boy come out of the jail. And George had Joe drive over to the court-house, and sent the rest of us to the hotel, tellin' Joe to drive back to Petersburg and tell Eliza where we was and what doin', and to keep everything a secret, so that Mr. Sprinkle wouldn't know about the Master; and to drive back to Virginia the next day. So that's the way it was. And after a while George come over to the hotel with a man, which was the judge of the county court, and he had supper with us. They sent me to bed, and I fell asleep wonderin' what would happen termorrow."

## CHAPTER IX

"THE next mornin' at breakfast I saw
Hardy Kirby for the first that I remember,
though he had lived in Petersburg onct. He
was wonderful, bein' tall and slim and strong,
with black curly hair, and a complexion like
a Indian peach; and he said the funniest
things you ever heard, and told the funniest
stories. So George was talkin' to him about
comin' to Petersburg to defend me on account
of the pie, and George and Charley for
breakin' the furniture. He said he would
do it and that he would make Mr. Sprinkle
look like a sprinklin' wagon when it has run
out of water, and jest drips. This was not
where Mr. Kirby lived; he had only come
here to court; and the judge was here, but

171

not of the court where we was goin' to take the Master.

"Finally we walked out and met the sheriff, and he said the Master had come to and was ravin' and threatenin' death to everybody, and prayin' and sayin' that he would call plague and fire and flies and frogs down on this town and on George and on me. He seemed to be awful bitter about me, the sheriff said. So then George went again to see the judge of the court which handles lunatics; and he made out papers, and they sent over to the jail and brought the Master before the judge. He looked awful. His eyes was bloodshot; he was pale all over his face as Miss Siddons where she was splotched; his hands trimbled; he looked around wild; he looked at George as if he was half afraid of him, and he looked at me long and stiddy as if he was sayin' a curse on me. Then he looked at the judge. So then the judge asked him what his name was, because George didn't know it and I didn't, and the Master said that his name was Jesus; and he folded his hands and bowed his head, and looked down at the floor. So the judge thought a

minute, and he said to the clerk of the court,
'Just entitle the proceedin's "The People
versus John Doe." So the clerk did some
writin', and then the judge asked the Master
if he had a lawyer; and the Master said:
'Think not that I could not presently summon
more than ten legions of angels that would
keep me from harm; nevertheless I open not
my mouth.' The judge now looked awful
sad and kind toward the Master; and as for
me I never felt sorrier for anybody in my
life; not even for Miss Siddons when she sang
'When Other Lips and Other Hearts' there
on the deck of the house-boat. The judge saw
that he didn't have a lawyer; and jest then
Hardy Kirby came in the court room, and the
judge asked him to defend the Master; and
he wouldn't because he said he was a friend
of George and mine, and was goin' to have
business for us and that it would not be right.
The judge agreed with this, and sent for a
lawyer. And meantime the jurymen come in
and took their seats and waited for the case
to begin. I was about as excited as I could
be. The Master was still standin' in front
of the judge, and the judge told him he

173

could set down; but he said that he must
suffer and be insulted and scourged and lied
about, before the end, which was soon near;
but after that would be the judgment when
the heavens would open, and the world would
be on fire and the good would be safe in
heaven; and then the gates would be shut on
the evil doers, and God would set the world
on fire and burn everybody up, except those
He had saved. So the judge jest let him
talk; but the sheriff was watchin' him and
the Potter boy, and George so as to grab
him. He had been searched before this but
they found nothin' on him but a small Bible,
a brass cross, and a copy of the St. Louis
paper. The judge had also sent for doctors;
and pretty soon the court room was full of
people, the word havin' gone around about
the Master; and the lawyer came who was
goin' to defend the Master, a Mr. Kimball,
a fine man, who did the best for the Master
all through the case.

"The judge now said to the Master that
he'd better set down and when he wouldn't
the judge told the sheriff to set him; so the
sheriff laid hold of him and set him down;

174

and the Master just submitted sayin' that he
would not open his mouth. Then the jury
was swore to try the case and George was
swore to tell the truth; and then the Master
spoke up and says, 'What is truth? . . .
what is the truth?' in a kind of whisper like
Sir Francis Levison does in the play when he
was plottin' agin Archibald in 'East Lynne.'
George told all he knowed and said in answer
to the state's attorney that he thought Mr.
Doe, which they called the Master, was out
of his head; and then the Master jest smiled
superior, as if he thought that George was
a poor thing and a liar besides. Then Mr.
Kimball cross-questioned George, and George
was jest as kind and nice as he could be; and
if I hadn't knowed him I would have believed
anything he would say, he was that convincin'.
Then they swore me and put me on the witness stand; and I told everything I knew
from the day I first saw the Master to the
day that he went away to St. Louis to be
crucified; and all about his talk, and about
the ring and about his tryin' to walk across
the Mississippi; and about my drivin' Miss
Siddons back to Petersburg, and about his

readin' the Bible all the time and sayin'
that his life was devoted to truth and Miss
Siddons' to vanity and the world, and
what she called beauty; and about his
settin' all day in the garden, and fencin'
with the sword, and repeatin' poetry and
everything. And the Master set and looked
down part of the time, and part of the time
at me, his eyes blazin' fire and revenge. But
onct he seemed to come to hisself, and then he
said, 'Where are we? Is this me?' jest like
he did on the boat. Then the Potter boy
got on, and he told what he saw about the
Master at his house, and about his funny
actin' there and that so as not to have no
trouble with him they had put sleepin' powders in his coffee so as to get him to Virginia without his makin' a fuss and a fight.

"So now I knowed for the first what it was
that old Mr. Potter had took out of the
clock; and George told me after this that it
was powders which he knew Mrs. Potter had
for neuralgia, because he had sent 'em to her
a few days before by Joe one day when he
drove out to the farm. And George also said
that he had planned the whole thing when

he was settin' with the Master and the rest of
us there in his parlor, right after the Master
had come from follerin' me, because Mr.
Sprinkle told him to; and that he was not
goin' to take the Master to the court in
Petersburg and have it so that Mr. Sprinkle
would let the Master loose as kind of a revenge on George for me and the pardon of
the boys and all that. I think that George
was about as smart in this business as a man
could be.

"So then the doctors got on the stand and
they swore that the Master was crazy and
dangerous, and ought to be locked up.
That made the Master rave. He got up out
of his chair and yelled, callin' everybody
vipers and thieves and devils, and askin' God
to curse 'em at the last day, and to send 'em
to hell, and to never forgive 'em. And he
tried to take the case out of the hand of his
lawyer, which the court had chose to defend
him; and tried to ask the doctors questions;
and finally he called the judge a fool and a
criminal, and a disgrace to the county; till
the judge got tired of him and told him to
set down, and when he wouldn't the judge

177

said if he didn't he would punish him. Then
the Master smiled and waved a long sweep
of his hand and said: 'I dare your honor to
punish me. If you punish me you say that
I know what I am doin'. And if I know
what I am doin' you can't take me from my
work of savin' the world. You can't punish
a man who don't know what he is doin' . . .
and I dare you to do it. I am Truth and I
speak truth, and you have no power over
me.' The judge looked awful funny when he
said this; so the judge jest said to the sheriff
to preserve order, and the sheriff took hold
of the Master real firm and set him down.
Then the Master got humble again, and set
there like a shamed girl lookin' down at the
floor. Then the case was about to end because there was no witnesses for the Master;
and Mr. Kimball said to the judge that he
was satisfied the Master was crazy, which
made the Master say that he was betrayed,
but rejoiced in it because Truth was always
betrayed only to rise up more glorious than
ever. Finally he asked the judge if he
couldn't testify for hisself and the judge said
certainly.

178

"The clerk was jest about to swear him when the judge stopped it; and the Master said he would only affirm and not swear; so he got on the stand and the sheriff stood close to him to watch him and he began to tell his story. He told about his bein' a boy; how as a boy God talked to him but he didn't know it, and how one time when he was walkin' by a church he heard God say, 'My son,' and that he fell down on his knees and cried; and how some boys comin' along hooted at him, which was always the way the world treated the Truth. How this made him ashamed of the truth and of God, and he hid what God had spoke to him; and how that accounted for him not jinin' the church as a boy, because them boys hootin' at him when he fell down and cried hearin' God, jest like St. Paul did, made him afraid that if he jined the church the boys would laugh at him; and so he went on denyin' God and gettin' into sin worse than St. Peter ever did. He said that he felt the judgment of God on him all the time he was a boy, and heard Jesus say, 'Why persecutest thou me?' and that he took to bad ways to drown out God's

179

voice and Jesus', and read infiddle books and
got doubts into his head; and then he took
up with all kinds of things to keep his con-
science still, such as helpin' the poor, and
fightin' for justice and for good laws in Kan-
sas where he lived; and lecturin' and finally
becomin' a preacher, and then findin' there
was not enough money for him as a preacher
in them days of sin; and finally becomin' a
actor, and all the time havin' firm convictions
about whatever he was in and tryin' to run
other people on such things, when they warn't
the truth and didn't matter; and that this
kind of truth was always changin', while the
truth of God never did; and he told about
meetin' Miss Siddons long ago, only his claim
was that he was mean to her and left her,
and that she didn't leave him and refuse to
marry him; and that it was in repentance
for this that made him marry her when he
did, which was a great mistake as she was
the Witch of Endor and Mary Magdalene
all in one, and had ruined him, except for the
power of God; and that he met her in New
Orleans sick and alone and took her on the
boat to save her soul and get her well; and

that he had married her in the speerit, but it
was never a marriage and there never had
been any union between them, any more than
there ever could be between the truth and a
lie, or the vanity of the world.  And that finally when he was gettin' ready to go to St.
Louis and show the power of God that I
came to live with 'em, and that I was sent
by the devil; that I was a toad turned into a
boy, and the toad that had set at the ear of
Eve when she was asleep, and tempted her to
eat the apple, which was the devil made a
toad; and that he had to contend with me after
I come as well as Miss Siddons, who didn't
believe the Bible, and mocked the stories of
the creation of the world, the flood, and the
tower of Babel, and the chariots of fire; and
healin' and resurrection, and everything,
sayin' that they was silly lies, and was a
bother to men and women tryin' to see beautiful things and a beautiful world, and God;
and was jest tales of barbarians, which ought
never to be paid no attention to by nobody.
And so he went on rememberin' pretty well,
what I had heard Miss Siddons say too about
such things.  But what was funniest of all

he said that Miss Siddons and me began at
first to plot agin him, because I was in love
with her and her with me, and we wanted to
marry, and that he had watched us all the
time when we didn't know it and that it was
while he was watchin' us this away that he
suspicioned about the ring, and so got it and
throwed it into the Mississippi.

"Then he got down to where he went to
St. Louis to be crucified and save the world.
And here the state's attorney asked the Master suddenly, 'Why didn't you?' That
seemed to knock him over. He set still for
a long time, then he looked straight at me,
as if I had kept him from bein' crucified, and
his hands kind of twitched, and finally he
come out with it, that it was me that kept him
from it, that I was really the devil, which
had throwed him off, and that after he got
away from the house-boat he knowed that
Miss Siddons and me now bein' free of him
would marry, and so he come back to save her
from that sin, before dyin'. So then the
state's attorney looked at him keen and says,
'Now ain't it true that it was this house in
Petersburg, which your wife inherited, or you

182

thought she inherited, or would, that made you come to Petersburg?' That brought the Master to, and he set up and braced hisself, and looked at the state's attorney, and then he bowed his head suddenly, and said awful meek, 'No one is good but God.' And the state's attorney said, 'That's very true.' It was awful still in the court room; there never could be anything solemner than this minute there with the Master on the stand all broke and cryin', for he was cryin' now, after really confessin' that Miss Siddons' house kept him from obeyin' the word of God. I could see that the judge was sorry for him, and wanted the state's attorney to let up on him. But suddenly he turned right around and set up and began to argue, and to say that his time had not yet come, for if it had God wouldn't have allowed the toad to come to his house and tempt Miss Siddons, and throw him off that-a-way. And so I could see that he was lots crazier than when we was all on the boat together, as crazy as he was then; for there he seemed to have some sense some days, and here he didn't have a bit, and kept contra-dictin' hisself in the same breath. In jest

183

a minute he turned around and said that it
warn't Miss Siddons' house that kep' him
from obeyin' God, that he obeyed God. Jest
think what a mess this was: Miss Siddons
didn't really have no house yet of her own,
and here the house was figurin' in the case
jest as if she had. . . . So he went on to say
that he did go to St. Louis, and there God
told him to go to Pike's Peak, and he did and
clumb clear up where there was clouds, and
there he talked in lightin' jest like Moses
and that God told him to come to Petersburg
and save Miss Siddons. So he turned to the
judge now and wanted to know if he couldn't
see his wife, meanin' Miss Siddons, and the
judge jest shook his head. Then the Master
began to talk about devils; and onct he spoke
of a animal which he called a whaledoodle or
somethin'; and he said that emeralds and
jewels was the scales of snakes. He got on
to Miss Siddons again; and he said she
smoked cigarettes, and drank wine, and that
she used to have music played that would almost drive you crazy, and that she danced,
and loved to, in rooms as well as on the stage.
Then he turned right agin hisself and what

184

he had said before; for he said now that
when he first seed Miss Siddons that she was
the most beautiful woman in the world, and
almost drove him mad with love; and that instead of him bein' mean to her and leavin'
her as he had said before, he supported her
word and said now that she left him and
would have nothin' to do with him, and called
him a crazy fool; and that he swore revenge
and God told him to revenge hisself; and that
when he met her in New Orleans that he seed
his chance to get back at her, and marry her
and take her on the river, and maybe get some
money too; because he said now he knowed
that she must have somethin' left from the old
days, no matter if she was sick and draggin'
around with her face. And so God had punished him; and it didn't matter how good he
had been to Miss Siddons the thought that
was in his mind when he married her had un-
done all the good and made the marriage
what it was; and he wanted to know if the
judge wouldn't divorce him right now from
Miss Siddons; and the judge jest shook his
head. Then he seemed to go back over his
life again and to talk about hisself when he

was runnin' a coperation or somethin' called
Justitia, which was run to bring justice
everywhere in the world; and he was goin' on;
but the judge was tired and told him to get
down from the witness seat; so he did, bein'
tired and kind of cowed. And the judge told
the jury to go out and talk about their verdict with each other. So the jury went out,
but not long, comin' back with a verdict
sayin' that the Master was crazy.

"Then the Master said he would take the
case to the Supreme Court of the United
States, that he knowed the judges and could
get justice there, and also that he knowed
the president; and that these friends of his'n,
besides bishops of the church, and all that,
would never allow harm to come to him. So
the judge jest nodded and smiled, and they
led the Master out, the sheriff did, I mean,
with the Master kind of wobblin', his head
bobbin' back as the sheriff sort of pushed him
on, supportin' him too by his hand against
his back; and it was awful mortifyin' considerin' maybe what the Master had been, or
anyway what he thought of hisself. So I
set there and saw the Master go through the

186

door. It was closed then and the Master had disappeared for good!

"All of us went out in the yard now, and George was talkin' to some men, explainin' the case to them, and I heard him say that Mr. Sprinkle had sicked the Master on to him to make him trouble, and that he found the Master was crazy, and so brought him to court, and so that was settled. Pretty soon I seed Joe over by the hitchin' rack, for he had come back with the carriage for us. So he come over, and wanted to know what happened, and George told him, and I did some too. Joe jest looked like a collie that sees a rat and knows it's a rat. He never said nothin.' Then we all drove back to Petersburg, stoppin' on the way to let the Potter boy out at his house, and to tell old Mr. Potter and Mrs. Potter and the rest what had happened. Old Mr. Potter was sayin' that them powders was good for neuralgia, and everybody laughed.

"Eliza was almost crazy to see us, she had been so worried. And when George told her that the Master had been sent to the asylum she looked as if a awful load was took from

her, even if she did have troubles enough on
account of me, maybe. It got into the
Petersburg paper about what George had
done with the Master, and Mr. Sprinkle was
mad and said there was a trick to it, and
that he was goin' to look into it as soon as
he had time from the bank troubles and such,
and after attendin' to me and puttin' me
where I belonged, where I could have schoolin'
and discip-line, and become a worthy citizen.
So one day when George got tired of this
talk about the Master from Mr. Sprinkle, he
went right up to him on the square and told
him to his face that the thing to do was to
try to get the Master out, and to come for
him for puttin' the Master in, and that he
would be there ready to show that he was
crazy, and that Mr. Sprinkle knew he was
crazy when he sent him to George's house to
impose on George and maybe kill me or some
of the fambly. That settled that. Eliza,
maybe, had told Miss Siddons first about the
Master goin' to the asylum, and bein' in
Petersburg. Anyway George told her about
the trial, one evenin' when she was over. And
so I was waitin' to be tried myself for the pie!"

188

## CHAPTER X

"I WAS goin' to Miss Siddons considerable now to help her, though I could see that Eliza liked me better and better; and even when she didn't need me for anything and I was goin' to Miss Siddons she'd say, 'Well, come back as soon as you can, Kit.' Maybe her and George was goin' to adopt me.

"School of course had took up, even before I got back to Petersburg from the Mississippi; but I didn't go owin' to the trial that was comin' on any time; but Cora Dunleavy was goin'. Still Ernest was readin' things to me, and besides jest to be with him and with George was to be learnin' all the time. Joe was takin' care of the horses, the stable and the cows, and goin' to George's farms most

189

every day; and George always had considerable business. We was a happy fambly all together, and I was wishin' it would last forever. My pap come over to see me onct and talked to George. He said he was satisfied to have me live with George, as he had no place for me, and maybe I was earnin' some money and he hoped savin' it.

"Miss Siddons had decided that she was goin' to make her yard look jest like it did when she was a girl, when her pap was alive and spent money on flowers and things. It was a awful big yard, with a picket fence around it, except on the fur side which was by the wood, and a little pasture and was really country. There was no street there, but only the outside of town. In the back of the yard was sheds and a stable; and on the lawn was great big pine trees, and near the house lilac bushes and rose bushes, and tulip beds, and such as that. Nothin' had been done with these things for so long that they was all tangled and rotted down and made the place look hanted. The house was a great big house, two stories with a two-story porch, and must have cost lots of

190

money. So I was workin' for Miss Siddons, and she was around with me wearin' white gloves, and sometimes carryin' a rake or somethin', clippers or scissors. She had other men to work too, old Jackey O'Donnell, the funniest old Irishman you ever saw. He claimed that to whistle at a person was the most insultin' thing you could do, and meant somethin' terrible. So when the Carey boys would come by and whistle he would almost jump out of his boots, and then he would take after 'em callin' 'em hog boys, and devils. They would almost laugh theirselves to death and of course he couldn't catch 'em. He kept callin' me a dacent boy and that my pap was a dacent man, and so was George Montgomery, one of the grandest men in the world, he would say. Miss Siddons was havin' lots of fun watchin' Jackey; and when the Carey boys would come by and whistle she would have to turn away to keep Jackey from seein' her laugh. But Jackey and me got along fine; and I found that by praisin' him he would work faster. I did this at first honest, and then when I saw how fast he spaded when I praised

191

him I used to do it jest to see him make the dirt fly. So Miss Siddons saw this and she had to turn away to keep from laughin' in Jackey's face. In this way we was havin' lots of fun. One day when Jackey was not workin' I went downtown for somethin' for Miss Siddons and old Jackey was in the store tellin' somebody about a wonderful cave in Ireland, where a princess was shut up onct, and while he was tellin' this and was not noticin' one of the McHenrys, a great big man, got up close to his ear and whistled so loud that you could hear it across the square. Jackey almost fainted and took out a knife and went for him. And one day when he did not know it was me I whistled at him as he was walkin' along, and he jest stood up straighter than ever, and began to almost run. It was too much fun to miss; but that is the only time I ever done it.

"So I was workin' along for Miss Siddons, and with Jackey too, and finally we had the yard all cleaned up, and new tulips set out, and the bricks straightened in the walks; and Miss Siddons was gettin' so she would leave her veil off sometimes, and I could see that

it had healed places and maybe would get
well, even if her face would always be scarred,
and what some would think was ugly.

"One day when we was workin' together
she asked me if the Master had told in court
how he happened to leave off actin', and when
it was. I said I didn't remember exactly,
that he said so much and repeated hisself so
much, that I couldn't remember. So she said
that it really happened when they was holdin'
a revival in New York, and it was near a
theater; and finally lots of people went crazy,
even actors; and it was decided that the
theater would be taken away from actin' and
turned over to God, seein' that a minister had
wrote the play which they was playin', and
which the minister took the money for,
though he wouldn't go to see his own play
on the stage. So the last night they was
goin' to use the theater for this play and
before turnin' it over to God to hold a other
revival in and save souls, the Master was
actin', and suddenly he throwed away his
sword, which was the same he had on the
boat; and he cried out that he was done with
actin', and would now go in for truth for the

rest of his life. Miss Siddons said that she
was in New York at the time, and everybody
was talkin' about it. But she said she didn't
really see the Master till later in San Francisco, when she remembered how he had been
in this here revival in New York. And then
the Master tried to marry her, but she
thought he was cracked; and she didn't know
why she ever married him even in New Orleans, when she really come to think about
it, except that if a man hunts a woman
enough maybe he will get her, and really is
pretty sure to.

"Miss Siddons all along was givin' me
things, and money too; and one day she gave
me a ring, with a blue stone and real gold,
and said she wanted me to wear it forever,
and that was part of what she would do for
me for bringin' her back from the Mississippi.
I didn't want nothin' really; for to be back
with George and Eliza was pay enough.
Miss Siddons warn't wearin' her veil now, and
so I could see her eyes, and I never seed more
beautiful eyes than hern for the color, even
if they was kind of pulled down, I mean one
of 'em was on account of the scars. For she

194

still had the red marks between her eyebrows
and down her cheeks, and under her eyes,
like that devil in the show that I told about;
but still not so red as they was; and the
crusts like the cherry pie was goin' away.
Dr. Walcott had been workin' on her all this
winter and spring, and had even tooken some
wax out of the skin of her face with a knife,
George said; and what they feared that she
might have a cancer warn't true. And even
if she was never very pretty again, she had
good eyes, and maybe her face would lose the
red marks.

"One day when we was fixin' some lilac
bushes she said that I had meant more to her
than most anything else in the world, and instead of bein' a toad I was a good fairy, a
good Irish fairy, and had been the most good
to her of anybody yet. 'How?' says I. And
she said I couldn't understand it; but jest in
a general way my comin' when I did, and
stickin' by her and gettin' her back, which
meant havin' George for a friend, and then
Eliza, and even poor Joe, was somethin' that
made her believe in things she had never believed in before, and maybe it was God. 'Why,

195

Miss Siddons,' says I, 'how could I desert you in all that trouble, you bein' alone and sick, even if I hadn't had that feelin' which come for not goin' over there on the Sangamon River and helpin' to get the body of Miss Douglas which was drownded. I couldn't have done it. One thing leads to another. And maybe Miss Douglas led to you. For how after Miss Douglas did I happen to drift right down to you there on the Mississippi, and you from Petersburg too, the same as me? I had to stick to you. It was in the cards, as my pap used to say.' So Miss Siddons said that maybe there was a God, but if there warn't I had been luck to her, and really was responsible for Dr. Walcott and all he had done for her, and what was better for the way she felt about people and things, better than ever before in her life; and even the loss of bein' a actress began to look not much and not worth worryin' about. This was the way she talked.

"I begun to notice now that Ernest Drew was comin' over considerable to Miss Siddons', specially when I was workin'; for then she would be in the yard, and George would

196

be off sommers and he would have no one to
talk to, Joe bein' busy and Eliza not wantin'
the men around until the end of the day,
when it was visitin' time. I would be rakin'
or runnin' the wheelbarrow, and Miss Siddons and Ernest would be settin' under one
of the apple trees talkin'. And when I was
off where I couldn't hear what they said I
could see Miss Siddons motion with her hands,
and shake her head, and sometimes laugh.
So I knowed they was talkin' interestin'
things, and that Miss Siddons was havin' her
say, which she always did, being' very posi-
tive in her opinions. Onct when I was
standin' near the tree where they was settin'
I could hear what they said; and Miss Siddons was urgin' upon Ernest that he was not
feelin' right about his trouble and that she
could make it all right for him if he'd let her;
and she laughed and said that she ought to
set up a advice office and tell people in trouble
what to do, because she had been through
everythin' herself, and knew how to advise
folks that was havin' trouble. I could see
that Ernest had some trouble too, and I had
thought all along he acted sort of quiet and

197

funny, and so this was it; but I didn't know what the trouble was, and wanted to. I was hopin' sometime he'd tell it to all of us. Because he knew my trouble, and Miss Siddons' and Cora's and Joe's.

"One evening the sheriff come to the house and told George that he wanted him to bring George and Charley from the farm; and it turned out that the judge had come and was holdin' court. So my heart kind of went into my throat for I suspicioned that my trial was close too. The same evening Hardy Kirby came to supper at George's, and he kept everybody laughin' with his jokes, and even joked me about the pie, and asked me if I was scart. I was, because by now I knew all about the Reformatory, and I could see that Mr. Sprinkle was as mean as a man could be. The next mornin' Joe went out to the farm and brought in George and Charley, but they didn't seem scart at all, and jest took things as they come. So I had to go down to the court too, and set around, as it turned out while they took care of George and Charley for breakin' the furniture in the jail.

198

"While we was all settin' there, me with the other boys and with George and Ernest, Mr. Sprinkle got up and told the judge that the two boys was in court who broke the furniture, and was ready to try 'em. Then Hardy Kirby wanted to know of him what he wanted to do with 'em; and Mr. Sprinkle said that was for the jury to say, and he was there to prosecute and not to fix the punishment. Then Hardy Kirby said he guessed he was there to fix the punishment or he wouldn't be forcin' a trial for such a little thing, and that the furniture didn't amount to much, not even ten dollars, and the way to do was not to take up the time of the court with such things, if there was anything more important like bank cases or Walter Rices to go for. This made Mr. Sprinkle awful mad, and he colored up, and flung back at Hardy Kirby that he was the state's attorney onct, and maybe not the most wonderful that ever was, to which Hardy Kirby said that he didn't have no chance when he had the office, that they didn't have no furniture cases when he had the office. And so they quarreled, and the judge cau-

199

tioned 'em to be polite to each other; but I could see that he was kind of laughin'. Finally the judge asked Mr. Sprinkle what the furniture was really worth, and he answered the judge by sayin' that so far as the value of the furniture was concerned that maybe ten dollars would cover it, but that there was a principle at stake, the same as if a feller tried to kill somebody, but didn't; and that they had broke the furniture out of pure meanness, and jest to destroy county property. The judge wanted to know how furniture happened to be in the jail where boys could get it, and Mr. Sprinkle said it was due to the goodness of the jailer who had tried to give 'em chairs to set down on, and that they had rewarded the jailer this-a-way. So then the judge asked Mr. Sprinkle if there was anything besides the two chairs, and Mr. Sprinkle said no; and the judge said that maybe ten dollars would cover what they was worth. Then the judge thought a bit and he kept lookin' at Hardy Kirby and Mr. Sprinkle, and finally he said, 'Where is the boys?' and Mr. Sprinkle pointed 'em out. And the judge said, 'Have

200

one of 'em come up here.' George Montgomery took Charley by the arm and told
him to go up to the judge, and he went,
lookin' as humble as a dog that crawls to
you. Hardy Kirby met him inside the railin',
and led him before the judge. 'I'd like to
ask him a few questions if you don't mind,
Mr. Kirby.' 'Ask him anything you want,
judge,' says Hardy Kirby, 'it's all right.' So
the judge had tooken the case in his own
hands, and he began to question Charley.
'What made you break the chairs . . . or
first did you break 'em?' And Charley said
jest as humble, 'Yes.' 'Well, what made
you?' asked the judge. 'We was mad,' says
Charley. 'What about?' says the judge.
'About bein' arrested for the pie,' says Charley. Then everybody laughed, except Mr.
Sprinkle, who seemed glad that Charley had
said this. Then the judge wanted to see
George Heigold, and he went before the
judge and the judge asked him why he broke
the chairs, and he said the same as Charley
had, with everybody laughin' as before.
Then George Montgomery went up before
the judge and asked if he could speak, and

the judge said certainly. So George told how
he had got 'em out of the Reformatory, and
was takin' care of 'em, and had 'em at work;
and that he didn't want the county to lose
anything and was willin' to pay for the
chairs, and didn't want the boys to have the
disgrace of bein' fined, or havin' any more
punishment for anything, and that he would
give ten dollars to the county treasurer and
end the whole business that-a-way. The
judge then asked Mr. Sprinkle what he had
to say to that; and Mr. Sprinkle said he
objected; and the judge wanted to know why.
And so Mr. Sprinkle started to make a
speech, and to say that the reason for crime
was that crime was not punished. That after
the state's attorney went to all the trouble
to get criminals into court, that then someone always come in to beg for mercy and to
bring in some old mother who was cryin' or
somethin'; and so criminals got off, and then
started right out to do somethin' else. And
that these boys was bad boys, and allus had
been; and that it was a shame on the county
that they had ever been pardoned; that they
had done lots of things besides the pie and

the chairs, and would soon be up to somethin'
else if they didn't know that the law was
strong and couldn't be stepped on. He spoke
of George Montgomery as bein' a well
meanin' feller, but clear wrong about crime,
and that Petersburg had got such a reputation that even lunatics was flockin' to the
town. 'You seem to like 'em,' said Hardy
Kirby. 'You sent one to George Montgomery sayin' that it was a good place to lay up.'
'It tain't true!' says Mr. Sprinkle. 'Well,
I have a witness who will swear that it is,
and he is in the court room right now,' says
Hardy Kirby. 'Come up here, Kit,' he says.
'So that's your witness?' says Mr. Sprinkle,
'the boy about to be tried for burglary.'
Then the judge said it made no difference
whether Petersburg was attractin' lunatics
or not, or whether Mr. Sprinkle sicked a
lunatic on George Montgomery; and he said
that he had heard enough. Then he asked
George and Charley if they meant to be good
boys now, and work and everything; and
they said they did. So the judge asked
George Montgomery if he would give ten
dollars to the clerk to give to the treasurer,

203

and George said he was glad to; and the
judge said to do it, and George did, and the
judge said to throw the prosecutions out of
court, and told the boys to go to their work
and be good and forget it. Mr. Sprinkle
was beat and couldn't say a word. George
Montgomery told 'em go up to the house
until after supper, and so they left, lookin'
happy and more theirselves than I had seed
'em.

"I was settin' there wonderin' what would
happen to me; and Hardy Kirby was havin'
a talk with old Mr. Ott which was the county
surveyor, as I knowed; and they was lookin'
at a map or somethin', when Mr. Sprinkle
said he was ready to try me, callin' it the
O'Brien case; and the judge asked Hardy
Kirby if he was ready, and he said he was;
and so they made me come inside the rail and
set by the table, and a lot of men come into
their seats, bein' the jury, and Mr. Sprinkle
asked 'em a lot of questions about knowin'
me or my pap, or knowin' George Montgomery, or Hardy Kirby, or ever hearin'
about the burglary, or havin' any idea about
it, or believin' whether I had broke in the

farmer's house or not; and whether they believed in enforcin' the law, or in lettin' criminals go scot free; and if they had ever been
arrested their ownselves or had a relative
who had; and whether they would listen to the
witnesses, and if they would foller the judge
on what he said the law was, even if they
didn't like the law, as he told it to 'em; and
more things than anybody could remember.
And finally after excusin' a Irishman from
near Rock Creek, who said that he didn't
think it was much to steal a pie, and some
others, the state's attorney said the jury was
all right, and turned 'em over to Hardy
Kirby to question.  Here somethin' funny
happened.  For Hardy Kirby said the jury
was all right with him; and so George who
was settin' there said that there was two men
on the jury that he wouldn't trust, because
they was close to Mr. Sprinkle in church work
and would do whatever he wanted 'em to.
But Hardy Kirby jest laughed and said it
was all right; and George leaned back in his
chair as if he was afeard that Hardy Kirby
was too certain, and might get fooled.  So
I could begin to see that I was in my lawyer's

hands and that he could do anythin' he wanted to with me. I couldn't do anythin' for myself.

"Well, then the jury was swore to try me, and they called the witnesses. The two farmers come who had cotched us, and swore that they seed us tryin' to break in the front door, and that's how they happened to come over to the house; but that we give up that and went to the back door, where they watched us until they seed us break in, and then come for us. Then the storekeeper came and testified that the cigarettes that they took off George and Charley was the kind that he sold; but when he started to answer Mr. Sprinkle's questions and say that his store was broke into the night before the pie was stole, Hardy Kirby said that wouldn't do, and jest as the judge was about to say that it wouldn't do, Hardy Kirby said to let it go, and so the storekeeper answered that; and said that his store was broke into the night before, but he didn't know who did it, and that he didn't believe I did it, or George or Charley because he had reason to suspi-cion another feller; but had no evidence.

206

I said I didn't, and never could know; that
I'd never heard of it until after this trouble
come up. All the time Mr. Sprinkle was
objectin', but the judge said that my name
had been slurred by this talk of breakin' in
the store and he was goin' to let me deny it
and swear to it. I looked at George now
and then, and he seemed to be worried and
to be wonderin' what Hardy Kirby was up to.
There warn't much for Mr. Sprinkle to cross-
question me about, for I had confessed to
everythin', and so he jest asked me a few
things kind of mild and let me go. Then
Hardy Kirby said he had one more witness,
but he couldn't get him till mornin', and he
asked the judge to put the case over. Mr.
Sprinkle kind of snarled now and said, 'I
thought you was ready to try the case; you
said you was; and now you say you ain't.'
And Hardy Kirby said he was ready all but
one witness, and he hoped the state's attorney
wouldn't be too keen, as the case would end
quick enough for him. Jest then some other
lawyers stepped up, who said that they had
been waitin' for a chance to try a short case,
and they'd like to get in here and try it.

So the judge said all right, and as it was about time to quit anyway he would put my case off till mornin'. So he told the jury not to talk to anybody about the case, and to come back at nine o'clock. Everybody got up to leave then, with me walkin' behind George and Hardy Kirby, with Ernest, who was mad about the case and sayin' that it was a shame and showed what civilization was that there could be such things as a case like this here. I saw George lookin' at Hardy Kirby awful earnest as he was talkin' to him; and finally when we got downstairs into the yard, George bust out in the loudest laugh you ever heard; and they both laughed. So I edged up and says, 'What you laughin' at, George?' And George says, 'You'll know quick enough, Kit,' and then he laughed some more, tellin' me to go home and help Eliza. So I went on hearin' George and Hardy Kirby laugh again clear across the square."

## CHAPTER XI

"UP to this time you hain't heard much of Ernest, and you don't know his story. As I said he was goin' now considerable to see Miss Siddons, and talkin' with her; and also he was downtown a good deal and had got acquainted with lots of people, and knew the stories of people's lives about Petersburg. He seemed to have some money, or enough; for I saw him give Eliza money for board, and say that he couldn't pay for the fun of livin' with 'em, but only money for the actual things. And Eliza seemed glad to have him around, and he was friends with Joe, and good to Cora, and everybody liked him. And of course him and George was more friends than what brothers would be.

213

"Well, that night after we come back from court, George said to Ernest, 'Let's go over and see Julia a bit,' so I asked if I could go too, and he said, 'yes'; so we went leavin' the rest at home, because Eliza was tired, and Joe and Cora didn't fit in on this exactly like me. It was a wonderful moonlight night, warm and nice; and the apple trees was awful nice to set under, bein' still sweet from the buds. So we went over, and George hollered up to Miss Siddons that we was out under the trees, and she said she would be down as soon as she got her mother to bed, all in a happy voice, and seemin' awful glad that we had come. There was some cheers under the trees, which Ernest and Miss Siddons had used as I have told; and George and Ernest took 'em and I laid down in the grass and began to look at the stars and the moon, and listen to 'em talk. Ernest seemed to be pretty excited. But at the beginnin' he said that the Master stood for foolin' around with what people called the truth, and so goin' crazy; and Miss Siddons stood for gettin' hurted for tryin' to do fine things, get happiness or somethin'; and that

214

is always talkin' law and morals makes a boy miserable, and for what? For smokin' cigarettes and playin' a banjo and dancin'. That was law breakin' to do that. It was none of the town's business. They had as much right to hound him about church as he had to make 'em play the banjo, if they could, or dance, if they could. Suppose the smokers would get a law that everybody had to smoke whether they wanted to or not? Wouldn't that be silly? But these people are doin' jest that by botherin' other people about what is none of their business. Well, look what follers: they make Walter Rice mad for life, and he goes away and thinks all his life how he can get even, maybe, and have revenge; and revenge is somethin' like a ball tossed back and forth, the game is never done!' Then he says, 'Look what follered from this: the state's attorney is a two-by-four, and takes it into his own hands to say that Tallman and the best people here that get it from Walter Rice shouldn't be punished for their breakin' of the bank law; and if he had said that Kit ought not to be punished because he was hungry, or be-

219

cause he didn't really mean no harm, then
there would never have been this pie case;
for that's what he says about the bank, that
it didn't mean no harm in takin' people's
money when it owed more'n it could pay,
for it couldn't expect Walter Rice to do
what he did and so to be put into that
trouble which was extra for the bank. You
never heard a state's attorney sayin' that
a pie law was unconstitutional. What law
is Mr. Sprinkle breakin'? Why, some of
the same kinds of law that he is enforcin' on
Kit; for he says the bank law ain't a law
because it is agin the constitution. So what
is enforcin' the law? It is over the left
shoulder, and everybody with sense knows
it. There is too many laws, and too many
that don't mean nothin', and that ought
never to be made, and that nobody ought
to respect anyway and obey. The state's
attorney can't enforce all the laws; he
couldn't if he had a hundred lawyers to help
him. So it means that the legislature says
this here is a law, but when it comes to enforcin' it, it either can't be, or like the bank
case here ought not to be; and sometimes
220

a higher law is obeyed when it ain't, jest becuz it is naturally right and sense not to obey it. So all the state's attorneys pick their cases, and have to. And Mr. Sprinkle, who is so good, and a church deacon and all that, picks his cases, too. So it makes law enforcin' silly, and a man who talks it, and makes a religion or somethin' of it is jest a fool or a bad egg.'

"Then Ernest begun to talk about Mitch Miller bein' kilt, and he said, 'Supposin' Mitch was knocked under the train by the brakeman, and that's the talk everywhere, is that somethin' for the state's attorney to look into? Could there be a meaner thing, a wickeder thing than that: to knock a boy under the wheels jest becuz he was stealin' a ride? You'd think from the way Petersburg acted toward that, and the state's attorney, that it was all right to take a boy's life for stealin' a ride; jest as it was all right to make a world of trouble and world without end for Kit O'Brien and his chums for stealin' a pie. Nobody has done nothin' about Mitch Miller and nobody cares. And that ain't all. Can you explain the state's

attorney bein' so active agin the boys jest
because they stole the pie, or ain't it to
get 'em out of the way, so that Mr. Miller
won't have evidence to sue the railroad? For
these law enforcers know that when George
and Charley go to prison, and Kit does, that
their word before a jury that Mitch was
knocked under the train wouldn't go so good,
and that they could be asked when cross-
questioned if they had ever been in jail, and
so be disgraced before the jury, with the
railroad lawyer sayin' that a boy who stole
and had been in jail for it would lie, too.
That's the game of law, and that's the way
it's enforced. I believe this story about
Mitch bein' knocked under the train, for
I know my ownself about somethin' like
it happenin' in St. Louis. There was a
boy there named Holland who was flippin'
one time on a train in the switch yard; and
a brakeman saw him and hit him with a stick,
knockin' him under the train, where his arm
was cut off. Well, the boy's father brought
a suit for the boy agin the railroad, settin'
up this brakeman knockin' the boy off, which
made him lose his arm. So the suit was

the blue ribbon at the county fair for the
best hogs—lots better; and that she would
prove it to the people here so that they
would see and believe it, too. She said that
the other day she was downtown and was
standin' on the corner near the fine store
that Henry Green had built, who had also
built the fine bank building, and the water
works, and had always done everything for
Petersburg. And she said while she was
standin' there old Cap. Weaver come along,
and didn't know her, bein' more'n eighty;
and that she asked him who built that fine
store; and that Cap. Weaver said that it
was built by Henry Green who was onct the
richest man in Petersburg but had failed,
after doin' more for the town than anybody. And he said that onct Mr. Green
come along after he was poor, and old and
sick, and stood on this very corner lookin'
at the store, which he had owned onct; and
he told Cap. Weaver that more'n twenty boys
had been named for him, includin' a nigger
boy; and that when he failed and lost his
money all these boys' names was changed,
except the nigger's. And Miss Siddons said

227

that Cap. Weaver said that finally Mr.
Green died and was buried and to this day
there was no monument to him. Miss Siddons said that Cap. Weaver told her all
this, jest as if she was a stranger in Petersburg, and didn't know some of the story herself, anyway about buildin' the store and
the bank and the water works. So she
asked George and Ernest what kind of people was it who would treat Mr. Green that
way, and what law was broke, but the high-
est law that people can know about, when
a man like him was treated so; and that not
havin' memory for a good man and not re-
turnin' good for good, broke the greatest
law in the world. And she wanted to know
if that kind of acts comin' from the town
didn't make this act of allowin' Mr. Green's
grave to be without a stone; and that she
had already gone to work to raise money
to put up a stone to Mr. Green, and had
writ a letter to old Mrs. Green that she was
doin' it, Mrs. Green bein' a old woman now,
and livin' in a other town with some relatives. Then George Montgomery said that
he was as bad as the other people here for

not havin' thought of this hisself; but now that Miss Siddons had started it he would give money, too, for Mr. Green's monument and would be glad to. And Ernest said the same.

"Then Miss Siddons said that Mr. Sprinkle was really the voice of the town, and was either doin' what the town wanted him to, or else by sufferin' it to be done, was the cause of the case agin me and the other boys about the pie. And that if you took some blue paper and put some acid on it it would turn red; so that you could tell that red was really in the blue. And that you could tell what the people of a town was by lettin' somethin' happen, and then see what the people would do, if they turned red, as you might say. And that if they was the right kind of people here they would not allow the pie case to be. She said that the rules that people made for theirselves was their ruination; and that she could prove it by somethin' she knowed which happened here when she was a girl. 'There was a girl here,' she says, 'who was goin' to marry a young feller, a very nice man he was, and

229

the girl loved him terrible. So one night
they was havin' a oyster party downtown,
and some of the men had some hard cider,
it bein' a time when the churches had voted
out the saloons. So this young feller drank
some of the hard cider, and got tight; and
the story went all over town, and made lots
of talk that this feller was tight. The girl
heard about it and spoke to him about it
and he said he didn't mean to, and wouldn't
again. But the girl's mother went to the
preacher of the church, and asked him what
the girl ought to do, if she ought now to
marry this man; and the preacher said she
shouldn't, that havin' got tight onct he
would again, and so might be a habitual
drunkard; and she ought to take no chances
marryin' such a man. Well, then the mother
went to the girl and told her she couldn't
marry him; and the girl begged and said
that she loved him and would be more un-
happy without him than she could ever be
with him, even if he was drunk sometimes,
which she didn't believe he would be. But
the mother said she had to obey and break
with the man, and that it was her duty to

obey her mother who loved her, and to obey
the preacher, who knew what was best and
right; and the girl cried and almost went
crazy; and finally the father come into it,
and they took the girl and sent her away, and
so broke it up; and Miss Siddons said that
she saw that girl for years after and that she
was always sad, and no good; and that
the man did take to drink, and in that way
proved the case for the mother, which he
might not have done it if he had married
the girl. So Miss Siddons said that it was
better to love a drunkard and live with him,
than it was to have no one to love, and to
live by what someone wanted who made you
do it, but really had no interest in your life,
after you was grown like this girl. And
she said there was nothin' but ignorance and
hate at the bottom of all this, and not a
bit of love or peace, or sense or good will.
Miss Siddons said that if the town could
be combed, or opened up and looked into
that you could find the whole thing jest
rotten with all kinds of foolishness and meanness; and that the worst of it was it passed
for a civilized community, but if it was civili-

zation didn't amount to much. And as for herself she thought she had been blind, too, except that she did hope she had never been mean, or without heart; if she had she hadn't meant to.

"Then George went after the newspapers, sayin' that they was the worst thing in the whole world; and that all a man had to do was to buy some type and a press and set up for a boss, and a ruler, and spread scandal and meanness all over the country. He said that they was allus hidin' what would hurt some man of their own kind, and printin' what would hurt people who couldn't defend theirselves; and that it was like some kind of magnifyin' power for human meanness; that hate and envy and cruelty and schemes which would jest be nothin' but one man walkin' about the streets and tryin' to do somethin' and maybe not able to, was in the hands of a man ownin' a paper some kind of giant powers able to ruin and to waste, at the same time that the owner of the paper was hidin' behind his paper and makin' of hisself a kind of god that you couldn't see or get at. That it was like one man be-

comin' the whole people, and speakin' for
'em, or speakin' maybe for this here civilization that they had been talkin' about, and
so makin' it strong and the whole force in
the town or country. And about hidin'
things in the paper, he said that he knowed
somethin' on Mr. Sprinkle, which was that
before he was elected state's attorney, he
was practicin' law and lendin' money here;
and that onct one of the Berrys, a widder
woman she was, livin' on a small farm near
town, wanted to borrow some money. So
knowin' Mr. Sprinkle for a deacon and a
good man she come to him for the money.
He told her he didn't have it; but could
get it from Ed Lane which was also a deacon;
but she would have to pay him a commission,
as Mr. Lane wouldn't loan money without
a commission. She wanted $700, and the
commission would be $100, and the interest
6 per cent. So she said all right to that;
and Mr. Sprinkle made out the papers and
gave her $600 finally, and she went away.
Then when the mortgage on her farm became due, her corn had failed and she
couldn't pay; so Mr. Sprinkle said he'd have

to foreclose and take her farm. That made her mad and she come to Mr. Brown the lawyer here, who knew what Sprinkle was up to, so he looked into it and found that Mr. Sprinkle had loaned his own money and hadn't gone to Ed Lane for it at all; and had got the $100 commission hisself, and the interest, too, and a fee besides for makin' out the papers; and so had really robbed this here woman. Well, lawyer Brown went to see Mr. Sprinkle, and as he was gettin' ready to run for state's attorney, and so enforce the law, he was scart, but at the same time insisted on his rights; and even allowed the case to be in court, but not tried. Brown set up in papers that Sprinkle had done this here, and there warn't a paper in town that printed it; and finally it was all settled without evidence in court and no one much knew much about it. It was brought up in the campaign, but was not noticed; because the churches was supportin' Sprinkle because he was agin the saloons and promised to prosecute 'em and close 'em up; and make Petersburg a moral town.

"'A moral town,' says Miss Siddons,

'wouldn't that turn wrinkles into dimples and smiles? It looks to me like more crimes are done for money than anything else: not by breakin' into stores or into screen porches, but by sneakin' and schemin', and by workin' the Presbyterian entrance.' So she said maybe she'd compose a song and call it, 'Teacher, Teacher, What Makes Me So Happy at the Sunday School?'

"Then George come back to newspapers, again, and he said that years ago, there was a man come over from a near town and wanted to start a saloon in Petersburg, there bein' saloons here at the time; and that the mayor, which was a good man, wouldn't let him have a license, because he had run a saloon in this other town where lots of bad men loafed, and there was lots of trouble, and also bad stuff sold. So this here feller havin' a little money went out and seemed to accept his medicine; but pretty soon they seed here a printing press and boxes on the depot platform, and then Joe Williams was haulin' these to the upstairs over the furniture store; and it turned out that this feller had bought these things and made a editor

235

of hisself, and was startin' a paper, which
he was; and also had turned a prohibitionist,
and was playin' with the church people,
which was glad to have him on their side.
So he called his paper *The Lance*, and took
for a title, 'The Home Agin the Saloon,'
and went out and made a awful fight on the
mayor and the saloons, too, and the billiard
parlors, and the fair grounds where they
had races when the fair was on; and on cards,
and on sellin' chances for prizes, such as
watches, or on allowin' people to guess how
many beans they was in a jar and so winnin'
a suit of clothes or a set of harness. And
he won out so that there warn't anything
goin' on in Petersburg but lendin' money,
and prosecutin' Joe Pink for beatin' his wife.
And George said that lots of papers was
started this way even in cities; and by men
who wanted to get back at somebody; and
that when these things happen there is more
big thievin' goin' on, and more rottenness in
gov'ment than at any other time. 'For,'
says George, 'you can take it the world over
that people that is jest havin' fun ain't
hurtin' nobody except maybe theirselves,

236

which is nobody's business, even if the good business crowd does say that it makes taxes higher and so bothers them to keep up jails and fool-houses; while this good crowd is doin' what makes poverty and makes the whole country rotten, jest from what is called business. Take me,' says George, 'I am looked on here by lots of people as kind of a fool, and by some as a dangerous citizen, sympathizin' with crime, and by some as havin' no business sense. Yet I get along, don't I, without lendin' money to widders and such as that? And I say that it makes money for the state to keep people's feelin's from bein' stirred up by law enforcement and war and all that, when it costs so much even to try a pie case; and so I say that they are the fools and not me. They pride theirselves on havin' the only sense there is in the world: but take the war business: there's more steal in that for army contracts than almost anything, and it is kept up by men who is always sayin', 'prepare,' 'prepare.' Well, you prepare, and keep it up and where are you? It may be years before there is a war, and you keep pre-

parin'. Well, jest as bookkeepin', which
would be better to do, this here, or to get
ready when the war comes? It would be
cheaper in money to get ready when the war
comes; and as for loss of life what is that
to fellers that is always talkin' about the
blessed privilege of dyin' for your country?
That bein' the thing to do, and a mere
nothin', anybody not willin' to die, or afeard,
is not worthy to live; and how wonderful
it is to die in battle, and maybe have
a monument of yourself for your children
or relatives to look at, with you carryin' a
gun and rushin' into danger, and so givin'
to your relatives somethin' better than
money, your life give for the country. Well,
now after lots of talk like this there is goin'
to be a fight now and then, the same as
two men quarrelin' will bring on a fight; and
the funny thing is to see these same people
who have been talkin' fight and how grand
it is, bein' so surprised when it comes, and
so mad at the other side for fightin', so un-
just and criminal and mean and low to want
to fight and so to kill; yes, to kill, which in

some of their talk is all right, because it is
wonderful to die in battle. Well, I remember an old feller that lived here that hated
the South in the Civil War, and was allus
talkin' of fightin' 'em, and givin' his sons
to battle if the war come. When it come
his sons went, and he went around prouder
than anybody; and finally when one of 'em
was kilt he jest raved, and called the South
murderers, sayin' that they had murdered
his son, and he was callin' for vengeance
and for God to burn, destroy the South;
when he had got exactly what he had been
hollerin' for as the grandest thing in the
world: his son had been kilt in battle, the
great prize had been won, and not only
that he had got what he might have expected; for somebody is bound to get kilt
when the war comes. And this old feller got
so excited, and grieved so that he died after
his son's funeral here. You see what fools
these people is when you really look into it,
both on arithmetic and everything, and if
the world warn't so rich that you can't
bankrupt it, and so full of people bein' born

all the time to take the place of them that dies this foolishness would ruin the world and these people would be showed in their foolishness and the control of things took away from 'em, and turned over to us who couldn't be foolisher if we tried. I don't think Slick Taylor or any half-wit could run it worse, or anybody that could even add up a row of figures. So I say that it ain't Petersburg that is a fool, and has no thoughts, but the whole country; and that nearly everything that gov'ment does this-a-way is foolish, and worse than any man of sense who was half tryin' would do!' And Ernest said he thought so, too.

"This is about the last I heard. I begun to get sleepy now lookin' at the moon through the leaves of the apple tree, and listenin'. Till finally I kind of cried out; for I was dreamin' of the sheriff comin' for me; only when he got close to me it was the Master with his sword, and we was down on the Mississippi. So then George come over to me and says, 'What's the matter, Kit?' And I kind of set up, and Miss Siddons said it

240

was time for everybody to go to bed; that
I had my case termorrow.  So they led me
over to where they said good-night to Miss
Siddons; and then we went home."

## CHAPTER XII

"THE next mornin' we was all up early, and Eliza was busy gettin' ready to go to court herself; and so was Joe goin', and Ernest, of course, who had been there before yesterday. George had left early because he said he was goin' to see Hardy Kirby about somethin'. Miss Siddons didn't try to go downtown with Eliza; but after we was all in the court room, and the judge had come I happened to look around and seed her, kind of in the corner of the room, where the light warn't so good; but I could see the red streaks on her face, like that devil I told about.

"That mornin' I heard George talkin' to Eliza in the kitchen, and he said that Hardy

Kirby knowed more people in Mason and Menard and Cass couties than any lawyer in a hundred miles around, or maybe anywhere; and that he knowed all about the land, and who had owned it, and all such as that from havin' so many land cases, when people was lawin' about boundaries and such; and that he knew all the farmers, and where most of 'em lived; and that there was no better man with a jury. Eliza looked awful interested in what George was sayin', but as if maybe George was spreadin' it on a little and was too confident of Hardy Kirby. But she was terribly afeard that I might have to go to jail; and she said that she wouldn't have that happen to me for anything in the world.

"The judge was on the bench now, and Mr. Sprinkle had come, which was lookin' fresh bein' all shaved and with his hair slicked back and parted, and his neck shaved, and actin' as if he meant to make things hum this mornin'. The man was at the table that was takin' down the evidence, and the sheriff standin' by the desk where the clerk was. So after a bit, with everybody still and waitin' to see what would happen next, the judge asked Hardy Kirby if he had his witness here, and Hardy Kirby said yes, and turned around and whispered somethin' to George Montgomery, who got up smilin' and left the court room. In a minute or two he come back bringin' Mr. Ott, the county surveyor, which I had seed Hardy Kirby talkin' to yesterday. So the jury kind of set up to see what was goin' to happen now. But before the case went on one juryman got up, and asked the judge if he could be excused for a minute before the case commenced and the judge said yes. This juryman was a old man, and looked as if he might be sick or somethin'. So the old juryman went out, and come back; and Hardy Kirby put Mr. Ott on the stand, havin' him sworn, the same as the others, and so began to ask him questions. He asked Mr. Ott if he knew the farm where Mr. Noel, the farmer, lived, and the farmhouse; and Mr. Ott said he did. He asked him how long he had knowed it and Mr. Ott said for more'n forty years. He asked him if he had ever surveyed the farm, and Mr. Ott

244

said he had; and when, and he said, 'About twenty years ago when your father had trouble with old Uncle Billy Jackson about the boundary.' Then Mr. Sprinkle interrupted and wanted to know if this here case of mine had turned into a land case, and what all this was about; and Hardy Kirby said to wait a minute and he would see; and the judge said to go on. Then Hardy Kirby asked Mr. Ott if he had looked over the notes of his survey, and he said he had; and if he had surveyed the property since twenty years ago; and Mr. Ott said he had, and done it yesterday, that is, surveyed where the house stood. Then he asked him if the house stood to-day just where it stood twenty years ago, and Mr. Ott said 'yes' to that. Then he come right out and asked him, 'Where does the house stand?' And Mr. Ott says, 'In Mason County.' Then he asked him, 'Is any part of the house in Menard County?' and I could see now that Mr. Sprinkle was twistin' in his chair and gettin' nervous; and when Mr. Ott says, 'There is no part of it in Menard County,' Mr. Sprinkle began to look around kind of

wild, and to cough nervous and swell out his
chest as if to ward off what blows was comin'.
I didn't know myself then what all this was
about; but I saw George smilin' from ear
to ear, and even the judge kind of smiled,
too. Then Hardy Kirby began to go into
it more, and he asked Mr. Ott where the
porch was at the back of the house, and he
said Mason County; and where the front
door was, and he said Mason County; and
where the front fence was, and he said on
the dividin' line between Mason and Menard
County; and where the yard was, and he
said all in Mason County. So then Hardy
Kirby said that was all he wanted to ask,
and he turned Mr. Ott over to Mr. Sprinkle
to cross-question; and Mr. Sprinkle got up
and went over to where Mr. Ott was settin'
and looked at the map, and finally asked
Mr. Ott where the atlas was, and Mr. Ott
said he would get it; and Mr. Sprinkle said
he needn't mind for the time; and he fiddled
around with Mr. Ott, and asked him about
the southwest quarter of the southwest quarter of Precinct 13, and all that and kept goin'

over it, till nobody could know what the thing was about.

"Meantime the judge set there kind of impatient; and Hardy Kirby was laughin' to hisself and finally whispered to George, 'Sprinkle acts like a duck that you've winged and which keeps flyin' around, gettin' closer to fallin' and comin' down every beat of his wing.' Then the judge says, 'Is that all, Mr. Sprinkle?' and he said it was, at the same time walkin' back to his seat, and facin' the audience, which didn't understand, the same as me what this was about. Then the judge asked Hardy Kirby if he had any more evidence, and Hardy Kirby said he didn't and didn't want any more; and then he asked Mr. Sprinkle if he had any more evidence, and Mr. Sprinkle said he hadn't; and then Hardy Kirby got up and asked the judge to send the jury out, that he wanted to say somethin' to the judge; and the judge said all right, and sent the jury out; and so they began to argue the case with the judge. Hardy Kirby first said that the crime of stealin' the pie had been done in Mason County, and it warn't the law to try me in

Menard County for a pie stole in Mason
County. And Mr. Sprinkle answered and
said that it was not proved that the burglary
was done in Mason County, because Mr.
Noel had swore that he lived in Menard
County; and that even if the surveyor, Mr.
Ott, did say that the house and the porch
was in Mason County it was for the jury
to decide whether the burglary was done
in Menard County and that it would not
be law for the judge to take it away from
the jury to say where it was done. The
judge kind of scowled now, and looked kind
of out of patience; but he didn't say nothin'.
Then Mr. Sprinkle asked to be excused so
he could get some law books; and the judge
let him, and he went out and come back
pretty quick with a whole lot of books and
began to make a speech. So the judge set
back as if he would hear everythin', and
jest give Mr. Sprinkle all the chance he
could. But I began to feel that I was pretty
near out of the woods, and to like the case
and to be havin' fun on account of it.

"Mr. Sprinkle would read from a book,
and then he would talk a while; and he was

off, and after floppin' around a little more he said that was all and set down.

"Well, I wish that I could set down all that Hardy Kirby said. He begun by talkin' of crime, sayin' that crime was breakin' the law, and that it didn't make no difference who broke the law, if it was enough of a law it was a crime; and that state's attorneys broke the law, too, sometimes. That they broke it when they was willin' to step on the law to send somebody to jail; and that while some people thought that a state's attorney could break any law in order to jail somebody who had broke the law, he didn't think so, and didn't believe the judge did. Then he said that there was men in Petersburg who was money lenders and broke the law not only of the books but of the Bible and the Church. At this Mr. Sprinkle coughed and swelled out his chest the same as before. Then Hardy asked what is crime? Suppose we did steal the pie, and suppose there was a principle at stake, didn't a principle call for brains to handle it; and in considerin' the principle warn't it necessary to consider the boys as

human bein's and all the circumstances,
either that or jest be Indians out huntin'
for heads? And this is where civilization and
morals comes in, he said. What is crime, says
he? Suppose we stole the pie, was it better to let the pie go or to ruin three boys
that might be men and good men in the
town? If there was principle at stake why
not get a case big enough for the principle, and not a pie that was too little for
it? Maybe the principle would fit better to
Walter Rice which had tooken $100,000 out
of Petersburg on his patent copper ex-
tractor. Why was nothin' done to him?
Maybe it would make too much of jokes
out of Mr. Tallman and the deacons here
to go into that. Why was nothin' done
to the bank that had tooken people's money
on deposit when the bank owed more'n it
could pay, which was agin this great thing
called the law, except that it was agin the
constitution, and this was what Mr. Sprinkle
was sayin' before any court was sayin' it?
How did he know that bank law was
agin the constitution? What is this thing
called law? he asked. Was it to be used
254

to help out the meanness, and the slander
and the selfishness and the littleness of people, instead of bein' used to really protect
the weak and to keep the town goin' up and
gettin' better? How you goin' to judge a
town, by the number of churches it has, or
by what the churches does? How you goin'
to see what civilization there is in a town
except by seein' what the town does when
somethin' happens? Supposin' some good
man or any man was murdered on the
streets, or houses was set fire to, and no
court took a hand, but the people was glad
that the man was killed or the houses burned,
what would you call the town but a Indian
town? You call this a moral town, he says,
and yet the governor lets these two boys out
of prison, and they come back here to live,
and to go on in life, and they are met by
the newspaper sayin' that they are burglars,
the St. Louis paper, which printed what
someone in this town must have wrote, and
by the Petersburg paper which prints the
same thing, too; and there is nobody here
to say that it is a shame and almost as bad
as murder, because it has that much hate

255

in it. Is that civilization, no matter how much law is enforced? Why didn't the citizens call a meetin' and pass resolutions agin the papers doin' this? They didn't, and that showed the town was glad that this was done, or too weak or careless to do anything. But if a soldier was brought back. the town would go wild and pass resolutions; and besides the whole thing was to have revivals and save souls by baptism, but never to save souls by treatin' people fair and true.

" 'Yes,' says Hardy Kirby, 'this is what you call a moral community, a community that fights crime; but when you get into it, you find it not carin' for real things, and full of hate and ignorance, and lettin' the game go the same old way, which destroys and does not save, compared to which the savin' of people in church is a joke.' Then he referred to Mr. Green which had been the banker here onct, as I have told, and lost his money, and went down from bein' the most respected man in town to bein' nothin', after havin' done more for the town than anybody who ever lived in it; and he had

256

## CHAPTER XIII

"THE next day and all along I was thinkin' what would have happened if I had gone to St. Louis the night the Master disappeared. Of course Miss Siddons would not have had me to drive to her home, but maybe she could have got somebody, and, of course, she could. Onct I was almost thinkin' that Carrie Douglas' speerit had got me to do this, knowin' I would get in all this trouble and bother without end, jest to punish me for not comin' over and divin' for her body. But still if a dead person would think that-a-way it would be no use to die; for that was less sense than to be alive. A live person would know better than that, and wouldn't be so spiteful. So that couldn't

261

be. At the same time it was comin' back that had made me so much trouble. Now I was waitin' for the never endin' case to get over, when I might be in St. Louis earnin' money and maybe havin' a good time. I could see what older folks meant when they said that nobody really knows what to do about nothin'. So one day I thought I'd go over to see Miss Siddons and ask her what to do, and if I shouldn't go away now, and so jest get out of everythin'; not that I was a cowherd, but I was tired and had enough of this here trouble. I didn't want to talk to Eliza, because she was busy and sometimes cross with all her troubles with all of us.

"George had warned me not to fight no boys no matter what they done; but in goin' over to Miss Siddons one of the Carey boys begun to call at me; and pretty soon another one come along and he begun to holler at me, too, and to call me Pie O'Brien, and the other one did, too. I wouldn't have done nothin' even now except when I come to the sidewalk where they was, they thought they could do anythin' they wanted to; so

they called me Pie O'Brien again and edged
up to me, one of 'em pushin' me. So I hit
him before I knowed, and the other one hit
me, and so we got into it, with me madder
than I ever was in my life. I knocked one
of 'em off the walk, and then I hit the other
one and made him spin, and they both started
to run, with me after 'em, until I come to
myself and let 'em go. Then I went on to
Miss Siddons'. She was glad to see me as
she allus was; and I begun right away to
tell her what was in my mind and about the
fight I had, and that maybe I would allus
be teased and taunted in Petersburg about
the pie. So she listened and then she begun
to talk to me. I was sayin' to her supposin'
that all my life they mocked me here about
the pie, the same as they did George Quinn,
who they called 'Ma' Quinn, because onct
when he got in the calaboose he sent word
to his ma that he was in trouble and wantin'
ten dollars from her, and sayin' 'Ma, come
to your boy which is in trouble.' Or supposin' I was allus teased like old Jackey
O'Donnell, or like Slick Taylor, the ijit,
what would life be but jest a torment all

the time? This is why I was talkin' to Miss
Siddons about goin' away. She said right
away not to run away, but to stick and
fight it out, and that there was a difference
between goin' away after a while when I
wanted to lift myself up in the world, and
runnin' away now when I ought to get the
trial over and everythin' finished. That she
had her face, and she was goin' to stick, for
what she could do here, and because she was
as well off here as anywhere, if she jest put
pride out of her head; and that's why she
was showin' her face now she had put pride
out of her head and she had somethin' better to do than to watch for wrinkles and
look pretty, even if she could. She said that
Ernest had runned away, and that was what
was the matter with him; that he had told
her all about it, and she had been talkin'
to him, and believed she had him fixed up.
Then I wanted to know Ernest's story, but
Miss Siddons wouldn't tell me. Then she
come back to the pie case, and she said that
things was finally looked at for what they
was, though it might be that while they was
looked at for what they was not it might

kill the person that was bein' looked at.
But that Aberham Linkern, which lived in
Petersburg onct, was arrested for violatin'
the flat boat law on the Ohio River, and
that it was so much forgot that only a few
had ever heard of it in these days; and that
the pie case would be the same with me if
I went on; and I would not be like 'Ma' Quinn
who never amounted to nothin' and so
couldn't get away from that story about
being in the calaboose and sendin' to his
ma for help. The way to live down anything was to be somethin' else, and to be a
different person from the one that had done
it. She said she was takin' care of her
mother and liked it, and that she would send
me away to school or do anythin' for me,
and that she would do it this very fall; for
havin' come back to her mother's home she
had more money than what she had before.
And she wanted me to think how lucky I was
to have so many friends, George and her and
Eliza; and that if stealin' the pie and runnin'
away to St. Louis had done all that for me,
which it had, that maybe it was as good as
goin' to Sunday School or anything else. Then

she told me to be careful about fightin' until I got out of court; and then to sail in and make the boys leave me alone; but at the same time to think and to act believin' that to feel friendly toward everybody was the way to live, that the trouble with the world was hate, and that the churches was as much up to hate as anybody, allus quarrelin' among theirselves about things that didn't amount to a pinch of salt, baptism and stuff; and that they was doin' right over again, and all the time what the churches did in Jerusalem, which fought Jesus because he fought 'em and showed 'em that they was spendin' their time on things that amounted to nothin'. . . . Well, we had a good talk under the tree; and finally I come back to George's havin' decided to do the best I could, and get through with this here somehow.

"Court was still goin' on, and Hardy Kirby was still in town, George said; and there was lots of talk about my case and the way it had blowed up for the juryman bein' sick, and people was wonderin' how it would end; and whether Mr. Sprinkle would let up on me. So pretty near a week after the trial, it bein' evenin', George and Ernest started out together, goin' down between the grape arbor to where there was a seat; and after seein' that they had went there, and as I thought set down I went out of the house by the side door and got down into the yard even with where I could see 'em among the vines settin' on this seat. So I walked along careful, and finally gettin' closer, got down into the grass, and sort of crawled along. I don't say that this was fair; but Ernest knowed my story, and I wanted to know his; and I made up my mind that when I got up to where I could hear 'em, if they was talkin' things that I oughn't to hear, and not about his story, then I would go away. So it was pretty dusk now and I crawled up through the grass and listened; and I was in luck for they was jest finishin' somethin' about Hardy Kirby; and then Ernest said that he had somethin' that he wanted to say to George. He said he had talked it with Miss Siddons, and she had give him some advice, and he wanted to see if George would advise him the same. So

267

George said what is it, and after a bit Ernest
began to talk. He said that he had a wife
that had drove him about crazy; that she
was the prettiest woman in the world and
in lots of ways the best; and that sometimes
when he would be settin' alone and thinkin'
that her face would come back to him and
he could see her eyes and the smiles in 'em
and her dimples, and could hear her voice
which was the sweetest voice he had ever
heard, and that it would almost drive him
crazy; and that this here had been goin'
on now for nearly three years; and he
wouldn't give in to it on account of pride;
and that Miss Siddons said that pride in-
terfered awful with what was best to do, and
had kept her from facin' things as they was
more or less all her life; that she ought to
have knowed long ago that she could never
do much with actin', and ought to have faced
it and tried for a different life; and that
pride had give her the face with the red
marks. So he went on to tell George that
while his wife was pretty and good and most
of the time was kind, too, that she would say
terrible things sometimes, when he was not

268

doin' very well about money; and had paid
too much attention to poetry, which had
allus bothered him to write, and which he
never would give up till he got hisself into
a state of mind like he was now where he
couldn't write it.   Because it couldn't be
written when a man was mad or sour or
havin' hateful thoughts, which had been him
for so long; and that you couldn't get clear
water from the spring when the turtles had
jest crawled through it and made it muddy,
so no more could you get beautiful thoughts
from a mind that was mad and sour and full
of bad thoughts.   Well, he said for a long
time he had gone on with his wife this-a-way,
lovin' her, and at the same time hurted by
her words, and bothered about money and
such things, until one day she said somethin'
to him, now worse than ever, sayin' that he
couldn't write poetry, and his pride got hold
of him, and he decided that he would jest
go away, run away like Kit O'Brien did,
he said, and that he did.   He went way
off at first into another city and got work
to do; and at first it seemed wonderful to
be free, and not to have his wife around him,

and not to have nobody to disturb his
thoughts; and so he got his books out and
read and wrote, and seemed to be pullin' hisself all together again, like a jint snake
which has flew to pieces and is jinin' itself
again; and he managed to send his wife
some money sometimes in a roundabout way
so that she would not know where he was,
and so to help her. Well, this went on, he
said. And then he got restless and began
to wander from city to city, and to kind of
lose hisself, till he didn't know what he was
any more; and that's the way he was when
George found him in St. Louis when George
and Eliza come back from their weddin' trip
to California. Then George said that it
looked like Ernest loved his wife and couldn't
get along without her without ruination, or
could, but it was like a man fastin', he
could stand it for forty days or so, sufferin'
like everything all the time, and then dyin'
or takin' food again. And that the thing
for Ernest to do was to swaller his pride
and go back to his wife; and he wanted to
know if his wife had asked him to come back,
and Ernest said not. Then Ernest said that

270

there was lots more to it than jest sayin'
he was goin' back, and goin'. That he
didn't know now which was his wife: the
woman with dimples and the sweet voice;
or the woman who hurted him with words;
and he was afeard that if he went back under the influence of hopin' to find what he
had loved in her that he would find what
he hadn't, and that would be the woman and
so he would be fooled. Well, George seemed
puzzled, for he didn't say nothin' now, and
nobody spoke for a while; and then George
said that there was more secrets in life than
anybody could ever know, and that nobody
was wise enough to judge anybody else; but
he said that Miss Siddons knowed as much
as anybody else and if she said he ought to
go back and try it again, that maybe that
was the thing to do; and that havin' tried
freedom and not makin' it work, maybe he
was ready now to find more in slavery than
he ever had before, and could do better with
it, and better than anything else. 'It's a
funny thing,' says George, 'how ambition
makes so much trouble; how it upsets judgment, and leads people away from their

families and everything, worse than whisky or anything; for when you come right down to it, ambition made all the trouble for Miss Siddons. It was ambition that made her fool with her face and so get it so that she couldn't show it; jest as some folks don't want to show their faces when they have no scars, but only bad thoughts within.' 'Well,' says Ernest, 'that's me. I feel now like not wantin' to see anybody. I hain't mixed much with people here; and if I went to the old places where people knowed me, I would not want to see 'em.' Then Ernest brought in somethin' else: he said that when he was jest up to the point of goin' back to his wife and sayin' to her that they couldn't live apart, that he had a scare that she might be changed, and wouldn't want him; and that he would see that he had come back to a life that he had destroyed; for he said that to leave anybody is to murder 'em, and that he had murdered his wife by destroyin' their life together, and leavin' it and goin' away. He was afeard now that she would not take him back, and there he would be, havin' give up his pride and she wouldn't want him;

272

and he would see anyway that the woman
he had left was not in the world no more,
that she was all changed, and he had been
led by the dream that she was there with
her smiles and dimples and sweet voice, only
to find that there was no such woman any
more.   Here his voice got pretty sad, and
George told him that he would have to face
the music the same as Kit O'Brien did in
comin' back to Petersburg.   And Ernest said
that he was more scared about facin' the
music than Kit O'Brien could be for the jail
and everything else.   Then Ernest said that
he understood Miss Siddons because her life
was the same as his'n when you come right
down to it; that she had allus searched and
so had he; and he begun to talk of a story
which the Greek people had made up, he
said, where a woman was so beautiful that
even God was mad at her, and started to
make trouble for her; and Ernest said that
anybody that was beautiful or smart or
tried to do somethin' got everybody mad
at 'em, so standin' for God.   And that this
woman was fell in love with by a god or
angel, maybe, who used to come to see her,

273

but she never saw him, because he allus come at night. But one night she lit a candle so as to see him, and he was asleep at the time, but some of the taller melted and fell on his shoulder and burnt him and so woke him up, and he scolded her for doubtin' and bein' curious, and then went away and she never saw him no more. And then God was mad and he made this woman go out and work and go from place to place doin' the hardest work, like scrubbin' floors and such, but all the while the angel was her friend anyway, and helped her bear her trouble, and finally she got God to love her again and went to heaven. So George said that this was the whole story about everybody who had an aspirin' nature: they drove the angel away that would have saved 'em at first and really loved 'em, and for that had to come down to work and humbleness to win back what had been their'n. So then Ernest turned right around and said that his case was lots worse than he had told it, and that what he had told was true about a year ago, but warn't now. And George didn't understand him, and asked him what he meant.

274

And this is what Ernest said. He said that
the wife with the smiles and the dimples and
the sweet voice was all true, and that it
was true that he dreamed about her, and
thought of goin' back to her; and that it
was all true that he had fears that she would
be changed, and that he might be fooled that
she was still the same and that he could
go back to what he had left; and it was all
true that he was tired of wanderin', and it
was true that his mind had got so that he
couldn't do nothin', and all that; but that
this was a year ago; and now he was in a
state where if anybody could tell him what
to do it would be like it come from God;
and so he said that this was the real truth.
He said that about a year ago in his wanderin' he got up to Boston, and was workin'
there on a newspaper and livin' in one room;
and some of the time goin' to a club where
there was a swimmin' tank, so to swim and
keep strong; and that this club was a place
where lots of young strong fellers come, and
older fellers that was makin' money in coal
and banks and such; and that there he got
acquainted with a business man who liked

him, a business man who had made lots of money in cotton; and that this man had come from the Ozarks, and havin' now made a fortune decided to go back to the Ozarks for the rest of his life. That this man liked him, and was good to him, and finally they was intimate, and became wonderful friends. And that finally, somehow he give this cotton man his confidence, because he was so troubled about his wife; and asked the cotton man what was best to do. He said he told the cotton man that he was afeard that he would find his wife all changed, or in a different mind, and changed to him, and her smiles gone, and her voice, and that it would be like goin' back to the dead, or findin' someone dead that you went back to. And the cotton man said that that was foolishness, that his wife would be tickled to death to get him back, and that she would be the same, only two years havin' gone by; and that if he didn't go back he was a busted man. And finally this here cotton man said that he would go to St. Louis with Ernest, havin' to go there pretty soon anyway on account of movin' to the Ozarks; and so he would go

276

now and stay with Ernest in St. Louis till he went out and made it up with his wife, that bein' where she was. So he said he got on the train with this cotton man and went to St. Louis, with the cotton man talkin' to him all the way, and assurin' him that it would be all right to do, and jest the thing. So he said that by the time he got to St. Louis he was pretty near wored out, and half crazy; but the cotton man was holdin' him up and tellin' him to go on, that it was his duty; and all the time it seemed to him then that the cotton man was better'n a brother in goin' with him clear to St. Louis and takin' all this interest. So he said the cotton man stayed at the hotel in St. Louis while he went out to see his wife. Well, his wife was glad enough, and did receive him and take him back; and it was true that she was changed, and didn't smile the same and her voice warn't the same, and she had changed to a older woman and harder lookin' maybe; but Ernest said that by now he was in a blur, and besides havin' gone this fur could not back out. So he went to the cotton man again back at the hotel and told him it was all

277

right, and thanked him; and then took up the
life he had left when he had runned away.
Then Ernest quit talkin' and it was all still,
with jest the air stirrin' in the leaves, and a
dog barkin' off sommers; and George said
nothin' and I was tryin' to think how George
was lookin', whether at Ernest or what. Till
finally George said, 'Well, what happened,
Ernest?' And Ernest said that it was more
than could be told; that it was more awful
than anybody could tell; that his wife's face
the next day was worse to look at than Miss
Siddons', because he could see that she was
a dead woman, and he had killed her, and
now had brought himself back, due to the
cotton man more'n anything else to set in
front of a dead face. That she was a dead
woman, and had no life, no thoughts, no
strength, no mind; and her face showed all
this; and her voice showed it; and there he
was, and had made her this, and now had
brought hisself back to bear the punishment of livin' with the dead woman which
he had kilt; and so he said his mind went
back on him, and he runned away again,
and went to a room in a hotel, after givin'

278

his wife all the money he had; and that it was here he was that George had found him when him and Eliza come back from California. Then Ernest stopped talkin' and George didn't say nothin', and I was layin' there sorrier for Ernest than I was for Miss Siddons. And George said finally, 'Well, Ernest, you've got to do somethin' for yourself, and I don't know what it is; for it's no use talkin' about your goin' back to her again. You've got to heal yourself the same as Miss Siddons has, and let the scars go. Anyway, it's time for bed now.'

"The two men got up now and started to walk to the house, jest as George was sayin' that anyway Kit O'Brien's case would be settled termorrow; but how it was to be I couldn't hear even if George knowed and said. So I laid there in the grass a while, lookin' up into the sky, and wonderin' what everythin' was about, and about dead people and the hereafter; and so I fell asleep right there in the grass."

## CHAPTER XIV

"I DREAMED about everythin' in the
world that night there in the grass. I
dreamed of Miss Siddons; I dreamed of the
Master; I dreamed of Ernest; I dreamed of
divin' for the emerald ring and bringin' up
a green snake which bit me. I dreamed that
Miss Siddons and Ernest was married, and
I saw 'em settin' at the table face to face,
and her with her veil on. I dreamed she
took it off, and then I saw the red marks
like that devil; and that she laughed at
Ernest; I dreamed of Ernest with the Master's sword; and then I saw Ernest again
and he had the red marks on his face, and
they was wet with blood. I dreamed of
Ernest's wife, and that she was sayin' to
280

him that a dead woman knows as much as a live woman, and that she was dead, all white and stiff. I dreamed the world was afire, and that the sky was full of angels with candles flyin' around, as if they was lookin' for somethin'. And finally I woke up, and the sky was jest gettin' yaller from the sun comin' up; and it must have been about four o'clock. I was cold and stiff, and I set up and rubbed my eyes and looked around; for the voices of the angels was still in my ears, and all these dreams was with me yet. I didn't want George to know where I had been; so I walked to the front yard and laid down; and finally I went in, and went up-stairs and got in bed, undressin'. George heard me and asked me where I had come from, and I told him the front yard; and he said somethin' to Eliza about me bein' a funny boy. So then I went to sleep again, and didn't get up till breakfast was ready.

"No sooner was breakfast over than George said to me to come with him. I didn't know what was goin' to happen, but whatever it was I wanted it over. Ernest was goin', too; but Joe warn't. I almost wished I was Joe,

281

with his collie eyes and ears and no troubles. I looked at Ernest and his face was white, his eyes was red; he was a sad lookin' man. Eliza was all business this mornin'. She was goin' to the farm, and Joe was goin' to drive her; and so me and George and Ernest started off. And we went to the sheriff's office. As we got into the hallway of the court-house a old man came up, which looked as if he had been waitin', and he said that he was the man that owned the boat I had tooken on the Sangamon River, and that he didn't want to make no trouble about it, but wanted pay, seein' he'd never get it back from the Mississippi. So George was awful hurried; but he asked the man what the boat was worth, and the man said it had cost him about twenty dollars to make, and he'd like to have that much and didn't want no trouble, or to make no trouble for me. Then George took out money and gave it to this man, and he counted it and said it was all right and went away. Then we went into the sheriff's office.

"The sheriff was settin' there as if waitin'. So George said, 'I surrender the prisoner to you, bein' his bondsman, and so release my bond.' And the sheriff said all right. And he took me. Then George went out leavin' me there with the sheriff, who asked me when I wanted to go to jail; and so I didn't know what was up. In about half a hour the coroner come in with Ernest, and he kind of arrested the sheriff for havin' me; so the sheriff and the coroner took me up to the court room, with Ernest follerin'; and there was the judge holdin' court, and Hardy Kirby and Mr. Sprinkle, and lots of people in the court room; and what Hardy Kirby had done was to take out a haborcus for me, and this was it. The judge who was doin' somethin' stopped it, and asked Hardy Kirby if he was ready, and he said he was; but Mr. Sprinkle was objectin' to everything, and makin' a nuisance of his-self. So then Hardy Kirby handed up papers to the judge, and the judge looked and seed me, and asked me to step before him. Then Mr. Sprinkle wanted to argue the case, and he was sayin' that there should be a jury, that he had looked up the law, and there should be a jury; and that the

283

haborcus was not the law, but were agin the law. Finally the judge said he didn't want to hear no argument from nobody, and wouldn't; and further that if Mr. Sprinkle didn't have any cases better than this pie case it was the thing to close up his office and save the people taxes; and he told Mr. Sprinkle to set down. All the while Hardy Kirby was a settin' calm and happy, and not sayin' a word. Then the judge told me again to stand before him; and I did, lookin' as brave as I could; and so the judge without wastin' words said that he was goin' to let me off and end the whole thing. The tears come to my eyes, and I had to let 'em, havin' no handkerchief; and so the judge went on to ask me some questions. He wanted to know if I would ever do anything like this again, meanin', of course, to steal a pie, and break in a house; and I said I wouldn't, that I'd starve first; which made him smile, and say that he didn't believe that I would. Then he told me to be careful all the time what I did, to think first before doin' anything, and to have good companions, and to listen to George Montgomery, and to work,

284

and to study, and to make a good man of
myself. And I promised. Then the judge
said that he had seed the state's attorney
of Mason County and he wouldn't bother
me, and that the whole thing was ended forever. So the tears started again, and I
rubbed 'em out with my fist and stood there.
Then the judge said to the clerk to enter a
order dischargin' me for good, which was
done; and then Hardy Kirby come over and
put his arm around me, and George had tears
in his eyes, but was laughin', too; and he
put his arm around me; and jest then the
judge come down from his seat, and he took
my hand, and said that after bringin' Miss
Siddons home that I should be give a medal
instead of bein' lawed agin; and he patted
me on the back. So Mr. Sprinkle warn't
there, havin' disappeared; and Hardy Kirby
said, 'Where's Mr. Sprinkle?' So the sheriff
said in earnest, 'He's gone for a drink of
water.' Then everybody busted out laughin',
even the judge. Jest then Miss Siddons
come in, bein' late; and when she heard what
had happened, she was almost tickled to
death; so her and the judge got to talkin'

"And now I could go anywhere to school I wanted to, for both Miss Siddons and George was willin' to send me. And pretty soon George Heigold and Charley King come back to town to go to school, boardin' at George's. And Eliza took it as her life. This is all the story there is up to this time."

## THE END